Bertrand and Wally go to AMERICA

Bertrand and Wally go to America

ERIC CARROLL

Illustrations by Bryan P. Ceney

The Book Guild Ltd

First published in Great Britain in 2024 by
The Book Guild Ltd
Unit E2 Airfield Business Park,
Harrison Road, Market Harborough,
Leicestershire. LE16 7UL
Tel: 0116 2792299
www.bookguild.co.uk
Email: info@bookguild.co.uk
Twitter: @bookguild

Typeset in 12pt Minion Pro

Printed on FSC accredited paper
Printed and bound in Great Britain by 4edge Limited

ISBN 978 1916668 126

British Library Cataloguing in Publication Data.
A catalogue record for this book is available from the British Library.

To my grown-up grandchildren:
Angelina
Gino
Carlo
Dominic

BY WAY OF AN INTRODUCTION

In the *Bertrand & Wally Tackle The Clovehitch Virus Crisis* story, our two insect friends found themselves on a different planet in another time and dimension. Along with their pals Beryl the ladybird, soldier ant Serge**ant** Andy, and not forgetting that outrageously comical cowboy cricket – Wild Bill Hiccup.

They were joined by many millions of other Earthinsects, thus easing the apparent pressure of both a pandemic and a population explosion, which was evident at that time, creating a CRISIS.

After a while, Bertrand began to realise that in fact *too many* had left the home planet, leaving now a *scarcity* of insect life.

So, Bertrand decided to return to Earth and back to England. Besides, he had felt somewhat homesick for the old country. So too had Wally. And the others, their friends. They all made the decision at the same time to leave the alien planet. They left as a group to carry on with their old and familiar life as before, in their original environment.

Any book worth reading by children is also worth reading by grown-up persons.

Arthur Ransome

BOOK I

ENGLAND

CHAPTER 1

Any insect who saw him would take him for a somewhat sinister and certainly a mysterious character. A tall, black, imposing beetle. He wore a large, wide-brimmed black felt hat and an enormous black cape or cloak. He was altogether quite unquestionably – oh, indubitably, if I may so express it – thoroughly drenched in *black*!

He appeared, dragging a large black sack, which seemed stuffed to the neck with something or other that crisply 'rustled'.

This tall, black beetle stranger paused at the door of 32A Beech Tree House, situated at the base of a mature beech tree (of course!), south end of Lower Tinklewigglebottom Wood in the fair English county of Picklepompshire.

He knocked.

In the space of a gulp of air gulped, the door opened an itsybitsy, and a face peered out. The door gaped wider an itsybitsy more to reveal, in all his glory, a bright jewel beetle of the noble *Buprestidae* family, wearing a hard regal coat of iridescent blue and green. The majestic aspect, however, was rather spoilt by a damp, scruffy apron tied tight around the waist of this individual.

The lofty stranger had in the meantime dropped the sack at his side and, preparatory to making a speech, coughed significantly into a black-gloved fist. “Bertrand-Bartholomew Beetle Esquire, I may presume?” he intoned in a serious and solemn voice.

“Yes?” Bertrand whipped off his apron in embarrassment and hid it behind his back. “Just helping the wife with the washing-up,” he admitted ruefully.

Which of course was a downright *fib*! Married indeed! As all the locals knew, Bertrand Beetle was a confirmed, decidedly dedicated and permanent bachelor.

“So, you are definitely Bertrand-Bartholomew Beetle Esquire?”

“Yes.”

“Of the *Buprestidae* strain?”

“Oh, I am not a strain!” exclaimed Bertrand, sorely offended. “I am a species.”

“Species… or a specimen?”

“Species, assuredly. A specimen is something else entirely.”

“A species, then. Not a speck, nor a spectre, nor yet a spectrum. I’m relieved that that has been sorted out.”

“Not as relieved as I feel,” said Bertrand, wiping his brow with the apron he had hidden behind him.

“And this is Beech Tree House, number 32A?” continued the tall, gangly creature before him, speaking in low funereal tones.

“Yes?” returned Bertrand.

Like the last time, his answer was more in the line of a question. *Who is this tall, black stranger?* he wondered a little fearfully. *A funeral caretaker? A rent collector? A tax official? A tax inspector!*

"I represent, sir, Lucky Dip Dunkles," the stranger said next, much to Bertrand's surprise and relief. "Lucky Dip Raffles and Lottery Department."

"Oh, yes?" said Bertrand, his answer once again being a question.

"I have information, sir, of great import with which to impart," went on the other in the same serious, slightly sinister, tone, "as it is of direct consequence to you, residing at this particular address."

"Oh, yes?" Bertrand's heart began to pound and bounce about within his chest.

"Oh yes, indeed, sir, I do."

The longish black beetle drew himself up to his full dizzy-top height and mournfully announced: "You, sir, have won this season's lottery…"

"Oh, my Aunt Angelina!" exclaimed Bertrand, all of a tremble.

"…The Jackpot this season amounting to ten thousand faldooshes…"

Ten thousand faldooshes! (If you happen to be American, dear reader, one faldoosh is equivalent to two dollars, so we are speaking here of a lot of dollars – twenty thousand of them! (the sums being correct.)

"…Which I have here in ready counted cold cash." And the lottery representative pushed the large, black sack towards Bertrand, the lucky winner.

"Oh, my Uncle Puddingsquelch!" Bertrand was overwhelmed.

"I wish you joy of your winnings, sir, and bid you good day."

"But-but won't you come in and have a nice cup of tea?" pressed Bertrand, now in raptures of ecstasy. "The kettle boiled this minute."

"Quite irregular, against company rules, sir. Good day to you!"

And the tall, black beetle stepped back a pace and doffed his hat. That done, he turned and scuttled off in smartish fashion, being now relieved of his heavy load.

At the threshold of 32A Beech Tree House, a much-bemused Bertrand gazed wonderingly at the enormous black sack set before him. Absolutely crammed with lovely, crisp, fresh-minted faldooshes. All his! Ten thousand sweet-smelling smackers!

But wait! Better check. He had a quick peep in the sack to be on the safe side. *Yes, indeedy*, it was there in all its splendour, and he believed his own eyes.

His mind clicked automatically into *spend spend spend!* mode.

I shall be able to lay down new lino in the hallway, he realised with a thrill. *And replace that old wheezer of a kettle with a brand-new expensive one. Expensive? Such luxury! Well, why not buy* ten *of them?! Ha-ha!*

The full measure of his newly acquired wealth began getting a grip on him. Fresh thoughts swirled around to sink in. *Why, by Joe, expense is now no object*, he realised exultantly. *Luxury is what I can now afford. A new rich way of life – ha-ha! Ten thousand faldooshes!*

Now, fair reader, Bertrand-Bartholomew was long known as a rather staid and stuffy, though respectable and correct, sort who knew the meaning of 'decorum'. This was perhaps because of his time spent as a schoolmaster. So, if anyinsect could see him in this moment, they'd think him right off his rocker. For in utterly un-schoolmasterly fashion, he was dancing and jigging about his living room, upsetting chairs, a table and one or two lampshades.

All of a sudden, he caught his breath.

"But wait! Wait on!" he babbled happily to himself, giggling out loud. "I must tell my friend of my good fortune. I must go this instant and tell Wally..."

CHAPTER 2

Bertrand did not have far to go in order to see his friend, as Wally lived merely a dog stick's throw away in the tiny village of Much Chipping-In-The-Wold, where most of Wally's old school pals lived.

When Bertrand arrived in this normally quiet, peaceful and typically English village, he found it far from quiet or peaceful. There was such a commotion of noise, chaos and angry voices, he could scarcely believe his eyes or antennae.

Earwig toddlers and little beetle girls stood around, crying their eyes out. Parents were shouting and throwing legs about in a perfect storm of fury. Wasps and crickets buzzed and chirruped at the top of their voices, hotly arguing over some matter or other. While ants and horseflies ran and flew madly in circles, droning loudly at one another.

What for all's sake is going on here? was Bertrand's alarming thought. He managed to collar an irate earwig nearby, ranting at another earwig – presumably his wife – and she was apparently giving back as good as she was getting, the pair of them steaming with rage.

"Excuse me…" began Bertrand tentatively.

"What's your problem?" snapped Mr Earwig with a bucketful of indignation.

"No problem," smiled Bertrand pleasantly, "but have you seen Wally – Wallace Warrington – Wally Wasp?"

"Wally!" shouted Mr Earwig furiously.

"Wally!" screamed Mrs Earwig, with such venom that it's a wonder it didn't strike Bertrand down cold dead.

"Yes, Wally," said the beetle, his smile fast disappearing. "I wondered if perhaps you had seen him around."

"That mad hooligan! That tearaway scoundrel!" cried Mr Earwig, hardly able to control his anger. "The bane of our life, that wasp is!"

"Scourge of the village!" shrieked his wife, spitting out her words like dollops of poison. "Him and his loutish lot of pals! A scourge I tell you!"

"But why?" asked Bertrand politely. "What is the matter?" wondering what all the fuss was about.

"Why? You ask why? What's the matter?" stormed Mr Earwig. "Don't you know? Haven't you heard? Have you no ears?"

"I have ears, Mr Earwig," returned Bertrand, deeply offended, "just as you have ears, Mr Earwig. But all I hear at this moment is a lot of silly quarrels going on, and for what purpose I simply cannot tell."

"The bikes! The motorbikes!" screeched both Mr and Mrs Earwig.

A gang of them as it happened. Wally being their leader. An unruly mob of Much Chipping-In-The-Wold youngsters, roaring dangerously around on high-powered motorbikes. Driving the village folk daft and senseless, with their revving up and speeding recklessly about the Common. "Oh! And that dreadful noise," complained everyinsect.

"And look," they all cried, "here they come again!"

Sounding not unlike a million angry hornets, the bikers roared and raced through the village. Each motorbike's exhaust blasted out one terrific BANG! as the riders skimmed past the petrified villagers.

And into the nearby meadow the bikers shot away like cannon fire.

"They'll be back in the shake of a leg," Mr Earwig informed Bertrand, who wondered which leg a beetle or an earwig could shake, for there are a number from which to choose.

So, in a shake of a leg – or a lamb's tail for that matter – Wally and his motorbike gang came rushing recklessly back to the Common.

CHAPTER 2 AND A HALF

When Wally's motorbikers zoomed away out of the village, an idea swiftly formed in Bertrand's nifty fertile beetle brain. He put it to Mr Earwig and a gathering of villagers. They readily agreed and promptly put the plan into a prominent and perfectly pleasing position.

It was a devilishly devised device to be sure, a deterrent without equal. What the villagers did, on Bertrand's clever advice, was this:

They quickly gathered up and stretched out an enormous tangle of spider's web – found draped over a bush by the bug pond – and stretched it tight across the main village street. Tightly secured (or securely tightened, whichever whatever) at one end by the bug pond and the opposite end at the Beehive & Bottle Inn.

All was ready.

"That'll stop their capers!" beamed a satisfied Mr Earwig. "Let's see them do a hundred miles per hour after that! Hee! Haw! Haw!"

The unmistakable sound of fully powered bike engines woomphing and revving told of Wally and his cohorts returning.

CHAPTER 3

"Oh, my marbles!" gasped a hairy caterpillar. "I do believe we're going to catch some *fish* in that there net!

The lead bike – Wally's, of course – plunged into the rigged spider's web, unsaddling Wally and throwing him into the clingy mesh. Then, every noisy, mucky, dangerous motorbike soon became enmeshed in sticky strands of web. The riders too, it goes without saying.

Wally and his pals were covered in a thick veil of webbing, and the more they struggled, the more tied-up they became.

There is nothing like English village wit to lighten up the day, and the Much Chipping-In-The-Wolders were no exception as they gathered round the hapless bikers.

"All tied up for the minute, are ye?"

"Are ye the spider's dinner or tea?"

"Not high tea, that's for sartin', hee hee!"

"Ye can let go of the brakes now!"

"What a *luvverly* catch of small fry!"

Wally, face red with acute embarrassment, spotted Bertrand in the crowd.

"Hi, Bertie!" He grinned foolishly and not a little shamefacedly. "How are things with you?"

"Fine," smiled his friend, "but not as fine as that web wrapped around you. You *wally*! What a *fine* specimen you make indeed!"

"He's in deep bother, brother," said a grasshopper nearby, "for look who's coming!"

"It's old Farmer Miles," said Mr Earwig.

"Come to sort out these noisy bikers, I'll wager," put in a worker ant. "All that engine noise has frightened his prize bumblebeef."

"Why can't these creatures stay at home?" suggested someinsect in the crowd.

"And play quiet computer games," said another, "instead of polluting up the countryside with their infernal racket and smelly exhaust fumes."

"Better make yourselves scarce, you bikers," advised someinsect else. "Old Farmer Miles is showing a face like a hot red squashed tomato!"

"Make yourself scarce, Wally," said Bertrand, as he helped his friend out of the tangle of spider's web. "Follow me, dear soul."

"Right behind you, Bertie, just lead the way. I'm not exactly welcome here for the present."

"You need to disappear somewhere for a good while," said Bertrand. And he knew exactly where and how.

CHAPTER 4

He soon shared the news of his remarkable lottery win – which delighted Wally no end – and decided also how to take full advantage of the immense wealth which was now his to enjoy.

Bertrand wished to visit America. He wanted to see his cousin Barnstorm who lived in New York City; and to visit another cousin by the name of Barleybean, who had made a home in the cowboy country of America's Southwest.

"Didn't Billy Hiccup's nephew emigrate to that corner of the world?" asked Wally.

"Wild Bill Hiccup, yes, his nephew lives there too, where my cousin resides. Same town, which I find an amazing coincidence, and not to say also a splendid convenience." He went on: "You see, I propose that we shall be taking Wild Bill with us. Hmm, certainly, as it suits admirably."

"We?" gulped Wally, wasp eyes agleam.

"Why yes, you would want to come along with me, wouldn't you, Wallace?"

"By pick a tick quick, I'll say! And I did… say," laughed Wally, pleased at this outcome.

"Well then, that is settled. Let us be off at once," said Bertrand.

"To America?"

"No, my dear Wallace, not right off at any rate, no indeed," smiled his friend. "Firstly, we need to pick up Wild Bill."

"If he'll come," countered Wally.

"Oh, he will come alright," confirmed Bertrand knowingly. "Wild bumblebeefs would not stop him from taking a trip to America's Wild West. We all very well know what Wild Bill is like when it comes to this cowboy stuff."

"So, we're off to…?"

"Uddersfield, my friend, Billy Hiccup's home roost. Uddersfield in gay Yorkshire."

CHAPTER 5

The two companions eventually arrived in the northern town, having travelled all the way by bus. Leaving the bus station, situated in the town centre, they were immediately struck by the quiet and peaceful aspect of everything.

Subdued, orderly crowds in the streets. None of the normal hustle, bustle and tussle seemed in evidence. No noise. No suburban upheavals, no friction, squabbles or quarrels.

An unreal silence reigned, but with an undercurrent of threat about it. Indeed (in insect parlance) it simply wasn't the same township anymore. So, what happened?

Bertrand tapped the carapace of a passing beetle.

"Excuse me," he began, "but why is it so quiet around here? Has someinsect of importance just died? Is a big funeral about to begin? I mean to say, it is not usually like this in Uddersfield, of all places."

"Aye, lad, tha's right theer," returned the beetle in a thick Yorkshire accent. "Used ta be a wild an' reckless kind o' town. And now – 'tis nobbut one big cemetery!"

The beetle shook his head in obvious disapproval and was

about to carry on quietly, and not a little fearfully, down the street.

"But why?" repeated Bertrand. "Why has it become so silent here?"

"No insect dare do owt," said the beetle with some indignation. "You do owt wrong here and you're liable to get your head shot off. And tha's a fact!"

"Are you speaking then of stiff, severe law and order enforcement in town at present?" said Bertrand, suspecting what he was suspecting. "Is that the case, my dear sir?"

"Aye, lad, tha's it in a walnut shell," replied the beetle. "That theer marshal o' ours thinks he's Wyndup Earp or summat like."

"Well, by my Aunt Angelina, what a fine bag of cornflakes this is turning out to be…" mused Bertrand.

"Aye, lad," agreed the citizenbeetle, "but nivver mind. Dunna worry ower it, cos the Council intend getting rid of yon marshal. An' soon, tha' knaws!"

The beetle continued on his way down the street, quietly of course and with head down low.

A short time later, as the two neared the town's municipal building, Bertrand discussed what he had heard:

"Sounds like our Billy Hiccup, without question – our Wild Bill has made his mark in no uncertain terms in this town of Uddersfield. Wouldn't you say, Wallace, my friend?"

"May be time he left town, I reckon," suggested Wally, perhaps thinking of his own misdemeanours in Much Chipping-In-The-Wold.

"I am sure he will be gone from here in the very near future," said Bertrand, "once I put my offer to him concerning America. He will surely jump at the chance."

"Which is what crickets generally do, as they usually do,

that is," grinned Wally. "Just as I can sting, when it is necessary, of course – now why have you stopped?"

"Why have I stopped here?"

"That's what I'm meaning."

"Here it is, my dear Wallace. The marshal's office no less. Hmm, yes, let us go in at once."

CHAPTER 6

"Bertrand has really gone and done it!" said Wally proudly, after the exuberant greetings and big-buzz-hugs and backslapping were over and done with. "Bertrand here has gone and won the lottery jackpot!"

Wild Bill Hiccup, the crazy cowboy cricket, still wore Stetson and shooting iron – or gun (or pistol!). There was only one difference, no small one by any means. For pinned to his chest was his badge of office, a marshal's silver star. However, there seemed no air of satisfaction about him, which Bertrand plainly perceived.

Wild Bill blinked and swallowed to digest the startling news just given by Wally. *Won the what? The lottery jackpot?*

"He has?" asked Wild Bill, wide-eyed.

"He has indeedy," grinned Wally.

"How much?" Wild Bill wanted to know.

"Sit yourself down first, Billy Hiccup," advised Bertrand. "Now, you tell him, Wallace."

"Tell me, Wally, old pardner!" pleaded Wild Bill, eyes wider still and eager and expectant.

"T e n t h o u s a n d f a l d o o s h e s," said Wally in slow time.

"Ten thou…!" Wild Bill burst into wild laughter. "Well! I'll be a hearin'-aided mistake-mappin' fault-findin' son-of-a-sawed-off shotgun! Fer a minute there I thought yer said ten – ten thousand – ten thousand faldooshes, that I did!"

"That's exactly what our Bertie Boy did win," confirmed Wally. "On the Lucky Dip Dunkles Lottery."

"Ten thousand faldooshes is correct," double-confirmed Bertrand. "In ready hard cash, in lovely crisp notes."

"Oh yeah?" queried Wild Bill, sceptical and disbelieving.

"Yes, indeed I did," triple-confirmed Bertrand.

"Yer don't say!" said Wild Bill, still doubtful.

"He just did," grinned Wally.

Billy Hiccup gave this some thought. *Why do these guys look so spruce and polished and prosperous? Why have they travelled all this way to see me? And – darn it! – why are they so all-fired pleased with themselves, as if they've won the lottery or something like?* Then it gradually began to dawn on him; it started to sink in.

"Ten thousand, yer say?" he persisted in a crafty voice, eyes glittering with greed.

"In perfectly clean crisp notes," said Bertrand with a smile.

Jumping up all of a sudden, Wild Bill let fly: "Dang it if I ain't a snap-happy joy-jiggered delight-diddlin' son-of-a-gold-digger! I'm rich! *I'm rich!*"

"Hold it right there, Billy Hiccup," put in Wally, with solemn face.

"Bertrand here won the money, not you, you corny cowboy cricket!"

"You – yer don't say?" said Wild Bill.

"I just did," smirked Wally.

"Broke!" moaned the other sadly. "Broke is this dollar-denied faldoosh-frozen, poorly paid money-mugged son-of-an-empty-pocketed-pauper!"

"And we're off to America," announced Bertrand cheerfully. "We are going to visit the great United States."

"We are?" Wild Bill's eyes lit up like a neon sign.

"No, *we* are," said Wally with a wicked grin. "Bertie and me."

Wild Bill's eyes dimmed all of a sudden, a darkly, lowly dimming.

"But you are more than welcome to join us," smiled Bertrand. "Which is why we came all this way to see you as a matter of fact. And listen here – *all* expenses are on me."

"Yeah?" Wild Bill's eyes lit up once again, and he slithered into a smug and slyly satisfied smile.

Bertrand explained his plan of first going to New York City to see his cousin Barnstorm, and then on to the American Southwest to visit his other cousin, Barleybean.

"Cousin Barleybean runs a hardware store down there," glancing at Wild Bill, "in a town called Tuxedo. I believe your nephew, who emigrated to the States, lives in the very same town as my cousin."

Wild Bill let out a laugh of delight. "Right you be!" he declared. "My nephew Will is holed up in a town of that name in the State of Arizona, near the border with Mexico."

"That is the very place, Tuxedo, Arizona," returned Bertrand with a high degree of excitement. "And that is where we shall ultimately head for, after first visiting New York City."

"All you need, Billy," advised Wally, "is your trusty pistol – fully loaded of course – your guitar and a portmanteau."

"Ha!" opened up Wild Bill, winding up a bit on the wild side. "No, Wally, no portmanteau fer me! What ah wants is a packsaddle! I'll be a trail-blazin' wild-westerin' Arizona-acomin' son-of-a-pickled-pioneer!"

"First things first, William Hiccup," continued Bertrand. "First, we need to pick up two more friends."

"You got friends!" popped out Wild Bill facetiously. He caught a severe, disapproving look. "Only kiddin'. Who'd they be then, these friends?"

"Why, daffodils-and-daisies, can't you guess?" put in Wally.

"I guess… no, I guess not."

"You careless clump of a cricket!"

"Yer mean me!"

"Such a half-baked muffin! We mean Beryl and Serge**ant** Andy!"

And so, a short time later, as they set off on their travels once again to meet up with the charming young ladybird and soldier ant friends, Wild Bill was positively steamed up with agitation. He was in fact becoming *wild*, hence his nickname.

In his obvious excitement, he told the others that this trip to America, firstly visiting New York City, reminded him of a lyrical limerick he'd picked up in Lower Lynerick. He whipped out his guitar and began to twang at the strings, his limerick going something like this:

"There once was a nutty grasshopper
"Through his own crazy fault came a cropper
"By the stupid and silly caper
"Of jumping off a skyscraper –
"And the bump on his rump
"Was a whopper!"

CHAPTER 7

The little market town of Knocktwice-On-Scrub was nestled in a tight U-bend of the River Scrub, in the small county of Wafflewendstone.

Wafflewendstone was squeezed somewhere between Lancashire and Cumbria. No one could say exactly where at any given moment, because Lancashire pulled and tugged one way, and Cumbria tugged and pulled another. Moved about in this most odd manner, the tiny county of Wafflewendstone was always considered 'unstable', to put it politely. Not that the inhabitants minded at all, far from it as the truth comes out, for it was always a nice free ride all round.

Now, am I digressing, fair reader? Scooting off the map? Yes, I suppose I am, a matter that ought always to be curbed. Where was I at?

Ah yes, I was relating about Knocktwice-On-Scrub. A really charming township of pebble-and-slate stone cottages, with lots of curious little shops. Shops of a rather old-fashioned, old-time bent. Shops with money tills that went *TING!* whenever the cash drawer was opened then shut. Shop managers wore elegant wigs; shop assistants wore bow ties and coat-tails, and all were extremely, and always, polite and ready to be of assistance.

It was the tradition in these parts. It should be emphasised that Knocktwice was, and still is, historically traditional and 'Englishsect' to the core, to the very bone marrow.

One of the town's redeeming features was the War Museum. Knocktwice itself had a distinguished war history dating back to the Crusades. The museum exhibits were housed in a handsome Tudor-Jacobean-Gothic building boasting three storeys – one above the other as you might expect. And the top storey was permanently reserved as living quarters of the curator-in-residence.

And the curator-in-residence at the Knocktwice War Museum was none other than that brave soldier ant, Serge**ant** Andy. Veteran of many campaigns, late of the 303rd Parachute Regiment, Royal Flying Ant Corp, militarily retired.

"Reorganising the filing system and reclassifying the museum exhibits, is without a doubt," muttered Sgt Andy, "without a single doubt a perfect *bore*! It's much too quiet and peaceful for my liking. By the smoking gun barrels I do miss the adventure and thrill of real active service!"

He glanced over at his secretary working industriously at a nearby desk. *Such a pleasant and engaging young creature*, he was thinking fondly. A ladybird (or lady*bug* – either way) in a million. As Sgt Andy had always maintained. He considered himself lucky to have her as his assistant and helpmeet.

"You're a gem, Beryl," he announced suddenly and earnestly. "You surely are."

"Oh! Oh!" flustered the ladybird, blushing hotly (all red with black spots!).

"No, what I mean is," Andy appeared equally flustered, "what I am trying to say is, there is a gemstone, a green-coloured one actually… named a *beryl*. Precious it is too… er hum, like you, pet."

"Oh! Oh!" again flustered the flattered female.

Then, right out of the blue, Sgt Andy popped out a question, by way of starting a further conversation: "I say, Beryl, how is your romancing these days, eh, pet? Doing much of it, are you? Courting, that is, hmm?"

"Oh, please don't let's talk of it," responded the female downheartedly. "I have quite sufficient already to contend with as it is."

"Only asking…"

The plain fact was, Beryl should have married this present season, but her beau had begged off and forthwith set sail for Africa. To discover new species of beetles, of all things! *And what about this little forlorn ladybird he had discovered here in England?* thought Beryl sadly, and not so long ago either. *Why go off hunting in faraway lands for what must always be total strangers, of all things?! Males! I shall never understand them*, thought Beryl in her near distraught mind.

"Yes, by the left-quick-march! Real action is what I need!" declared Sgt Andy with heat, entirely on his own track of thought. "You know, Beryl, my pet, in the war of '03 – or was it '02? – anyway, when I was—"

"Oh goodness golly me!" the ladybird interrupted him. "Is that the time already?"

"What's that you say, my precious?"

"Time for tea!" announced Beryl, leaving her desk. "I'll make us a nice pot of tea, Sgt Andy. You just sit at ease there and sort your firebombs from your 'thumpshells.'"

"Er, yes, right you are, Beryl. Crack on, my pet, smartly does it, off you go then, one, two, three, stomach in, chest out, chin up, shake a leg, shake them all, left-right, left-right!"

But Beryl was already in the kitchen, putting on the kettle.

CHAPTER 8

Later, over a steaming hot cup of tea, Sgt Andy freely and unendingly reminisced before his captive audience of one. Not, as you would expect, about his own extensive war experiences, but of his distant warrior ancestors. Great soldier ants all, such as Sir Ironball Smashem, The Black Baron, Lord Firefist the Elder and the honourable Earl Hitem-Where-Ithurts.

"And then, Beryl, just as the castle portcullis was halfway raised…"

"Yes! Yes!" panted Beryl in Great Expectation (good title for a book – or has it already been done?).

"You'll never guess who came riding in on their sturdy bumblebeef steeds," continued Sgt Andy, eyes twinkling with his own sense of enthrallment. "There were three of them, Beryl, only three of these riders—"

And at that very instant, the door opened and in clomped Bertrand, Wally and Wild Bill Hiccup, all three with beaming faces.

"Thundering carronades!" exclaimed Sgt Andy with

perfect delight. "If it isn't *Les Trois Mousquetaires*!" (Another good title for a book – or has it already been done?)

"We come in peace, Soldier," smiled Bertrand.

"Three *pieces* to be exact," grinned Wally.

"A born-again beetle, a whiff-of-a-wasp and yours truly – a crackpot crack-shot old crank-of-a-cricket – Wild Bill – Hiccup! – Beggin' yer pardon!"

Within the week, the intrepid travelling fivesome set sail from Liverpool Docks on a magnificent ocean liner, the *Queen Bellabessie*.

On they sailed over the vast ocean blue
To new adventures as they well knew,
And to meet new friends of every kind
In that Great Land which brings to mind
Of glories and stories that always ring true.
On they went
With eager intent
These five adventuresome few.

Queen Bellabessie

CHAPTER 9

As the Queen Bellabessie *was steaming well away from the Port of Liverpool, a tall, dark, mysterious-looking beetle stranger was rapidly scuttling along the quayside.*

When he learned only a short time later that the luxury liner had slipped its moorings some time back and was now fast progressing through the Irish Sea, he simply stood panting, trying to get back his breath.

"I have missed them!" he said to himself. "Those five insects beat me to it, and I almost had them in my grasp. Oh botheration! Oh vexation!"

He was exceedingly vexed and bitterly bothered to be sure. That big ship was sailing for America, to New York City. Which meant that he too was compelled to travel to New York City.

"I have got to get to America!" he said to himself. "I shall catch the next available ship; that is what I shall do. What I must *do."*

He rested awhile on the long stone quay, cursing his luck, which was non-existent.

Why was this tall, dark, mysterious-appearing beetle stranger so obviously desperate to catch up with our Famous Five?

Only he knew that...

BOOK II

AMERICA

ONE WAY

PART ONE

NEW YORK CITY

CHAPTER 10

"Here we are then, Wally, right in the heart of New York City, known colloquially as 'The Big Apple'. As far as I can ascertain, we are on 42nd Street at the corner of Broadway. This is Manhattan! And we could not be in a busier place than this, I am sure."

"It certainly is busy, Bertrand, and noisy too. What with all this traffic on the street and all these humans rushing and pushing about on the pavement."

"*Sidewalk*, Wally, that is the correct term here. Let us move to the curb edge before we get trodden into oblivion."

The two insect visitors were on their own, for the party had split up. Beryl, Sgt Andy and Wild Bill wanted a deal of time to have fun at the 'World's Largest Playground'. They desired quality time at the famed Coney Island. To enjoy themselves at Luna Park and Dreamland.

Of course, Wally would have loved to go with them but, being a loyal and faithful creature, he chose instead to stick with his friend. "Has your cousin given you the right address?" he now asked Bertrand. "How would an insect survive in this… this – whoops!"

A sudden gust of wind – a 42nder – set to rolling a

discarded paper cup. One of those pointed cone-shaped cups. It rolled in a 180-degree turn, sweeping Bertrand and Wally into the gutter.

They found themselves by an iron grid covering a drain, bumping into a young cockroach that happened to be there.

"Hey, New York ain't big enough for you that you have to butt folk out of the way?!" said the roach rep**roach**fully.

"My most sincere apologies, sir," blurted Bertrand, dusting himself off.

"Say, are yous guys out-of-towners? You sure look like out-of-towners," said the cockroach, now in friendlier tones. "Where're you from, fellas?"

"We are *out-of-country*, young sir, from England, to be precise, and I feel a long way from Lower Tinklewigglebottom," in an aside to his wasp friend. "Indeed I do."

"And I'm a long way from Much Chipping-In-The-Wold," chipped in Wally with equal sentiment.

"Well, welcome to New York," said the roach. "Come to see the sights I guess, huh? I'm Ed Crusher, by the bye, at your service."

"Most kind of you and many thanks," returned the beetle. "Actually, I am here to visit my cousin, if I can find exactly where he lives."

"Has he a handle?" said the cockroach.

"I beg your pardon?"

"What's his head from his tail, his moniker?"

"I beg your pardon?"

"Who is he? Has he got a name?"

"Certainly, he has a name. It is Barnstorm."

"*Barnstorm!*"

"It sounds very much like you may know him, or know of him."

"Barnstorm! Know him! Why, mister, everyinsect knows Barnstorm, the mightiest mobster in Manhattan."

"Mobster?" queried Bertrand in some alarm. "Are you saying that he's a gangster?"

"Yeah, sure, but not the type you might think."

"There is only one type of gangster I might think – ruthless, wicked and totally dishonest."

"All that hooey! Phooey! Just hold up, mister, you're getting it all wrong. Barnstorm is nothing like what you said there. He's a *Robin Hood* type of mobster, or gangster as you put it."

"A *Robin Hood* type?"

"Yeah, sure, that's right. You betcha! He robs the rich and gives it all to insect charity – well, most of it leastways, there's always expenses to consider. We're all insects, right? And some of us are in need of a bit of charity, a cut off the pile, eh?" A hard edge was creeping into the cockroach's voice.

"How splendidly commendable of dear Barnstorm," enthused Bertrand, smiling now with relief and satisfaction. "Well now, Edward—"

"*Ed*. Ed Crusher."

"Well, Ed, how might I find him, my cousin?"

"Easy as cheesecake. Right here. This is his spot, his plot, his own space."

Bertrand and Wally glanced about in some bewilderment.

"Here, you say?" said Bertrand, indicating the busy thoroughfare.

"Here this way, through this grid, guys. Follow me," and the roach disappeared down the drain. "Come on!" he shouted up from a ledge he had landed on. "Just jump!"

Bertrand and Wally took the plunge and jumped.

"Now this here chute you see before us," Ed Crusher began to explain in the dim light below the grid, somewhat cut off from the noise and bustle of the street, "this chute takes you all the way down to Second Level. That's where most insects live in this city."

"Is it safe? The chute I refer to," said Bertrand.

"The chute's safe, safe as Wall Street. Except mebbe when there's a flash flood. This chute takes away the floodwater, you see. We've had no rain for quite awhiles, so it's bone dry. Mind you, it might rain later; it is forecast."

The cockroach paused a moment, then grinned a mischievous grin. "This is the quickest way of reaching Second Level. Though there is one even quicker than this."

"There is?" Wally wanted to know, out of keen interest – he simply loved speed.

"Yeah, sure, buddy. Don't know if you noticed, but the grid across the street from this one is definitely the fastest. 'Dead Drop Drain' we call it. A dead drop all the way down. Not to be recommended, except for the foolhardy."

"We're not foolhardy," Wally pattered out. "Maybe a little foolish at times, me especially, but never foolhardy."

"So, what do we do here, Edward?" asked Bertrand.

"*Ed*. Ed Crusher. That's my tag; that's my label; that's how you crank me, but you can call me Ed. How do we get down, you were asking? Easy as slug pie à la mode, you get my meaning? You take a flying leap and you're on your way. Like this…"

Ed Crusher the cockroach took a dive and shot down the chute like a bullet.

"Wheeeeeeeee…!"

Wally went next. "Wheeeeeeeee!"

Bertrand shrugged a cavalierly, devil-may-care shrug. "When in New York, do as the New Yorkers," he muttered to himself, falling freely into the chute and down.

Into a wholly unimaginable abysmal blackness…

CHAPTER 11

A certain tall, dark, mysterious beetle stranger at last found himself in America. To be precise, in a shipping office in Brooklyn naval dockyard, New York City.

He was making enquiries with a far-from-happy expression on his face, speaking in forbidding, mournful tones as he made his enquiries.

"I wonder if you have seen or heard of a particularly peculiar party?" he asked of an earwig clerk.

"Peculiar in what particular way, this party, sir?" politely said the clerk.

"Well, I speak of a party of five individuals, each quite different from one another."

"In what way are they different, sir?"

"Well, there is a beetle, a wasp, a ladybird – or ladybug as they say over here – an ant, and a cricket."

"What a mixed bunch, sir."

"Quite so, I readily agree. The cricket by the bye wears a cowboy hat and... I believe he may also be armed."

"That is curious! And how many arms has he? No legs at all?"

"No, you misunderstand me. I mean he carries a pistol, a firearm, a gun of some kind."

"A dangerous one, is he?"

"I daresay he is, but perhaps only if you poke at him or say a rude or wrong thing to his face. At all events that is how I believe it."

"So, sir, what's your interest in these insects?"

"Well, actually, I am only interested in one of them. The beetle. The others just happen to be with him. Yes, it is the beetle I am keen to catch up with."

The earwig clerk took in the other's dark, unfriendly visage, his sinister aspect – one could smell *the sinister aspect. "Are you from the FBI?"*

"The Federal Bureau of Insects? No, I am not, not now, not ever."

"You're from England, then, or so I take it?"

"Exactly so, that is correct."

"Ah! The SIS perhaps?"

"The Secret Insect Service? No, not at all, at all ever."

"Then perhaps it's MI5 or MI6, yes?"

"No, I am nothing to do with intelligence or espionage or any secret service matters."

"Speaking of service matters, I'm afraid I cannot help you, sir. I have not seen these five individuals you mention, though I've seen many a number of insects pass by this office, mostly cockroaches I might add – off the ships, y'know, always off the ships." The earwig clerk ruminated for a moment and continued on. "As you are maybe aware, sir, insects ain't humans – not by any means, as you will fully appreciate. You see, insects, they can come and go, in and out of any country they please. With nothing to hold them back, no passports required, no visas, no legal papers of any description, no—"

"Thank you, clerk, you have been a great help! Good day to you!"

The tall, dark beetle stranger left the office like a severe thunderstorm.

He would somehow find those five insects. And that beetle *most especially...*

A fair time later, the black-hatted stranger was still questioning insects of many kinds on the streets of the city. Many of those he approached seemed to see him as a sinister sort of soul, certainly a suspicious type.

Then along came two police officers, big, black, burly stag beetles, who confronted him with some menace in their manner.

"What's your problem, bub?" asked the senior of the two, a sergeant, and to the English visitor, never was there such a browned-off looking, bad-tempered, beetle-browed beetle that here confronted him.

"No problem at all, Officer, merely making my enquiries of a private nature," returned the tall, dark stranger, and began to explain about his quest to find five certain insects.

"Who are you, bub? Where're you from?"

"My name is Mournmorrow. Silas Mournmorrow, of Graveside Hollow, Cemetery Lane, Dead-End Town, Expireshire, England. I simply need to find these five insects, or one in particular."

The police officers exchanged knowing looks.

"Got a right one here. How about it, Sarge?" said the less senior official, in what the stranger considered an alarmingly nasty and threatening tone. "Shall we give this rare plum a sample of our noted New York Police Department hospitality?"

It came as an unpleasant surprise when the black-hatted stranger – now identified as one Silas Mournmorrow of

Graveside Hollow, etc. – this unfortunate creature found himself hustled and hauled to the local precinct station, wherein he was promptly thrown into the lock-up.

His only consolation – which he hardly thought a consolation at all – was that he had the police cell entirely to himself.

CHAPTER 12

"Where are we?"

Bertrand and Wally, along with their new-found cockroach friend, were deep down in a dank underworld. The English visitors gazed large-eyed upon a massive open concourse, a 'Grand Central Station' of this remarkable subterranean world. The whole vast area was cast in a dim sulphur-yellow light.

"Kinda crummy down here, I know," admitted the roach, "what with the lousy lighting an' all."

"What a mighty load of traffic and insects!" observed Bertrand in wonder.

"This is New York City, pal," the roach reminded him.

"All going in one direction it appears," Wally could see. "As fast as they can go. These New Yorkers are sure in one hasty hurry."

"Yeah, that's a bit weird. Something's wrong here."

"The hustle and bustle," voiced Bertrand, "is that not normal?"

"Oh sure, but what I mean is – as your wasp friend pointed

out – everyinsect's going in the same direction. Or at least away from that far side there."

The roach managed to halt an earwig in his tracks. "Say, what's happening around here, bud?"

"It's Ratchett!" cried the earwig, eyes wide with fright. "Ratchett's on the rampage!"

"*Ratchett!*"

"Is there something we ought to know about?" asked Wally warily.

"Who might Ratchett be?" enquired Bertrand, with impeccable British politeness.

"Why, Ratchett is the… he's over there! Look!"

"Oh, my missing marbles!" gasped Wally.

Bertrand stared in horror, then found his voice: "*A giant rat! A monstrous rodent*!"

"You see its tail?" said the roach. "It's twice the normal length – even for a massive beast like him. He uses his tail as a… there! You see it! Using his tail as a whip!"

"He is whiplashing those poor insects," moaned Bertrand heavily.

"Spiders and cockroaches and beetles…" said Wally with feeling.

"Yeah, he's rounding them up," returned the roach. "For his next meal."

"What do you think we should do, Bertie?"

"I think we should stay put right here behind this girder, Wallace, that is what I think we should do. And stay quiet and still."

"Righty-ho! I'm with you on that score."

"Good thinking that, Mac," said the roach. "Best not to go out into the open and become an easy juicy target, for he's sure to see us."

The three of them peeped fearfully from one side of the iron girder in this underground darkworld.

"Oh look! How did that spider get caught?" whispered Wally. "It has all of eight eyes, yet it didn't see the rat coming."

"Ratchett was too quick for him, I guess," returned the roach. "And that tail of his is long and fast, greased lightning fast!"

"It's really quite scary."

"Yeah, you're right there, buddy. Scary as coughin' comin' from a coffin."

"How dreadful! Just look at that!" exclaimed Bertrand. "The beast is eating them alive! Crunching them between his teeth. How awful!" He was horrified at the grisly sight.

"Now he's heading for that main channel," said the cockroach. "Up above that would be Broadway proper. Should find some food scraps from the restaurants there. That'll stop him gobbling up decent living insects for a while, I guess."

"Is it now safe for us to move on?" asked Bertrand, cautious eyes wandering about the place.

"Safe for a stretch, sure… only…"

"Yes? What is it now?"

The roach was looking directly before them. He saw something else that didn't bode well for their safety or security.

"See those two heavies?" he whispered in dark tones.

"Rather on the large size, yes, I see them," acknowledged Bertrand.

Said Wally, "You couldn't miss them big fellows."

"Big trouble, buster, they're Bruiser and Brawnstone. Another sect of our Manhattan Mobsters. And definitely coming this way. Act like you're scared," advised the roach.

"No need to act," fluttered Wally. "I *am* scared."

"A stiff upper lip, Wallace," said his beetle companion. "Remember, dear soul, we are British."

"Oh we are! We are!"

"Ahh jeezjerry-jackleberry! They're coming right over to us! Us!"

CHAPTER 13

Nothing happened.

Those two tough-looking characters Brawnstone and Bruiser simply sauntered on straight past Bertrand and company, without so much as a glance at them, as if they were not there.

"Phewey!" cackled out the cockroach. "That was close."

"Have they gone?" came a new voice from behind the other side of the girder.

"Who said that?" queried Wally.

"That you, Boss?" said the roach. "Yeah, Boss, they've gone. It's safe to show your face, I reckon. I'm real glad to see you, Boss."

"Boss?" queried Bertrand, in an aside to his wasp friend.

"Ah, good, thanks, Ed," continued this new voice. "Can always count on Ed Crusher, eh!" And the owner of the voice came into full view.

He was a jewel beetle, a *Buprestidae*, just like Bertrand, followed by a small entourage of other insects, presumably his underlings.

"Barnstorm!"

"Bertrand!"

The two cousins eagerly embraced.

"Well, I reckon I've done my bit," said the roach, "so I'll shoot off, I guess."

"Many thanks indeed for your generous time and assistance, Edward," said Bertrand with typical English civility.

"Ed. Ed Crusher is my handle. Guess I'll see yous guys. See ya!" And the young, friendly cockroach scurried off and was soon out of sight.

"You're lucky to find me, Bertie Boy," said Barnstorm cheerfully a moment later, leading the way to another area of this dim nightworld, "because I'm on the lam, you see."

"*On the lam*? What in goodness is *on the lam*?"

"I'm temporarily in hiding, that's what I'm meaning."

"Are you perhaps in some kind of trouble with the police?"

"The cops! Jeez, I'm always in hot water with them. No, my present problem is the Muckrake Mob, the Westside Manhattan Mobsters. Hellraisers and Troublemakers, with a capital T. Anything bad around, they got it, they own it, they use it. Yeah, they're my headache right now, on account of a little disagreement concerning some rightful territorial rights, ya know what I mean?"

"I think I do…"

"I don't know what you mean," admitted Wally, butting in on the conversation.

"No matter an' not your concern, you limey wasp," sneered Barnstorm. (He had apparently taken an instant dislike of his cousin's companion, regarding him sourly.) "So, I'm on the lam, Bertie. Got to keep moving around, stay one step ahead of them – or three steps behind. Last night I was holed up at Cosh Cockroach's place," he continued explaining, "a nice warm kitchen at some spaghetti joint on 14th Street. Tonight, I'm staying at Bob Inn Bed Rest."

"Robin redbreast?" said Wally.

"Did I say 'robin redbreast', you oddball limey wasp! I said Bob Inn Bed Rest." Barnstorm turned to his cousin. "What's with your wise guy pal? A screwball or something? Where's he at?"

"Oh, don't mind Wally; he is just young at heart."

"Flung a dart, you say?"

"No, not flung a dart, *young at heart*."

Bertrand was eager to get his cousin off poor Wally's back and changed the subject: "It certainly is a busy place down here," he said, indicating an intense congestion of traffic and many insects hurrying hither and thither.

"Yeah, we're pretty well organised here," responded Barnstorm, somewhat complacently, as though he were entirely responsible – which might in fact be the case. "We have better systems than those humans up top; we're more efficient. Moreover, we're actually linked to New York's subway network. We can go to any borough we want – Brooklyn, the Bronx, you name it. And get this, it's all *free*!"

"That sounds most enterprising, Barnstorm. But how do you use the Underground – sorry – the subway lines?"

"Easy as snail slime pie, cousin. You face your *insectmobile* to a train carriage. Next, you switch into magnetic gear. Your vehicle rises some and then, SMACK! It's stuck flat to the side of the train. Once you reach your destination, you switch off the magnetic power and lower yourself to the station platform."

"That sounds simple enough, one would think," smiled Bertrand.

“Well, the thing is, you must hit your train smack flat straight or else.”

“Or else what?” wanted to know Wally.

Barnstorm glared at the wasp and made reply in a cutting tone: “If you hit off the straight at an angle like, you CLONK! instead of SMACK! Don’t hit it right and you wind up on the railtrack – getting fried on a million volts.”

“Ooo, that’s nasty,” replied Wally with a shiver.

“Yeah, yeah...” grinned the other, his mind evidently on some other track.

Bertrand too was momentarily *distract* (sorry, reader) distracted. He heard a distant clattering, metal-jangling, deep drumming, thrumming sound that was getting increasingly louder, and LOUDER... and LOUDER!

CHAPTER 14

Meanwhile, up above at street level somewhere in downtown Manhattan, a harassed beetle insect was peering questionably about him. He was tall and dark and kind of broody in aspect. An altogether sinister and mysterious-looking creature.

And released from jail only that morning. He was of course the character going by the name of Silas Mournmorrow, looking for a raindrop in a puddle, as the saying has it. Looking indeed for five certain insects, but one in particular, in this vast, crowded city.

He did not feel at all safe where he was, on a busy thoroughfare, and was nearly trodden on several times. "This will not do," he said to himself.

Then he spotted a little human boy, and the little human boy spotted him. He knew what little boys were like, knew what nasty, hateful things they were capable of. This singular boy did not in any way appear to be the exception. Far from it. He looked cruel, spiteful, malicious and quite dangerous.

The little boy was going to enjoy what he intended doing.

He kicked the insect, sent it spinning and skidding across the sidewalk. Now it was his immediate intention to stamp on the beetle, to hear it crack and squelch deliciously under his shoe heel.

Yes, the boy was definitely going to enjoy this bit of fun. But just as he raised a hard-heeled shoe, he was yanked back. He was with his sister, several years his senior, and she tugged determinedly at his coat sleeve.

"No, Henry!" she exclaimed. "I know what you're up to. It's cruel and uncalled for. Come away, we're late already for your piano lesson with Mr Steinwell," dragging her little brother away from the beetle insect on the ground.

"Phew!" breathed Silas Mournmorrow with massive relief. "But I simply must find that party that is so elusive… and set my sights on that beetle."

Like trying to find a raindrop in the ocean, *he thought with rising frustration.*

He scuttled across the sidewalk, to the streetside curb.

And dropped over.

Directly down a drain…

CHAPTER 15

The ground below Broadway trembled and vibrated and violently shook – as did all the insects. They were quite used to it, but not the visitors from England. Wally was caught off-guard and bounced about like a soft rubber ball.

The sound seemed to have solid substance and was now a great roaring monstrous thundering!

"What in goodness!" cried Bertrand, as he too bounced about like a bean in a bucket. "I am sh-shuddering! Oh, my Aunt Shirley, sh-should I be sh-shuddering!"

The horrific noise turned now to a distant rumbling clatter, the walls echoing its sound.

"What in goodness was that?" he asked Barnstorm, when at last the great din abated and he found his legs once again.

"Subway train," explained his cousin. "Maybe the Pelham 123. Directly above us, that's where the tracks run."

"I took it for an earthquake."

"Yeah, pretty wild and noisy, ain't they just," returned Barnstorm casually. "We insects only operate on this lower level, except for long travel trips. Pretty well away from human presence down here. It's where you'll find the flash flood drainage channel and sewage outlet," he continued to explain. "We also got access to the gas pipelines, electric cables, telephone lines and the rest of it down here. We use the humans' electricity for light and heating. There are loose wires all over the place, so it's easy to connect up power, ya know what I mean?"

"Yes, indeed I do. Most enterprising. You have it fairly well organised, I must say."

"That's right, Bertie Boy. Only the noisy subway trains to put up with, and the occasional flooding, but we can live with that. I guess our biggest headache is coping with that darned rat, Ratchett."

"I have already seen it in action," said Bertrand soberly, "and it would seem a massive problem for you all."

"Yeah, something needs to be done about him…"

A little spark of an idea began to grow and glow in Bertrand's clever beetle mind. *Maybe something can be done about that rat*, he ventured to surmise, *and the sooner the better.*

"By the bye, where is Wally?"

Barnstorm gave a short laugh. "He got bounced up against that maintenance cabin over there, see? He's coming…"

Wally came staggering back to them, weaving about with severe dizziness. "I'm all dizzy and dopey," he said woozily.

"Yeah, you said it, you limey greaseball wasp, dopey fits you like a glove," said Barnstorm unkindly.

"Your eyes are crossed!" burst out Bertrand with alarm. "You've gone cross-eyed! Can you uncross them, Wally?"

Wally managed to straighten his eyes. "Is that better?" for which Barnstorm gave him a sour look.

The Manhattan Mobster grabbed hold of a passing gangster-ish-type beetle.

"Hey, Luke, light me up a Lucky, whaddya say?"

"Okay, sure thing, Boss. Ya wanna chocolate, banana, lucky dip…?"

"Lucky Strike is what I want, you meatball!"

"Barnstorm!" cried Bertrand, aghast. "Do you smoke?"

"Only when I'm on fire."

"But… that little white stick, to me it looks altogether like a—"

"Aw shucks, Bertie, this here Lucky Strike is only a sticky toffee."

"Oh, I see."

"Ya want one, pally?"

"No thank you, I'm trying to give up such things."

"Uh-oh!" voiced one of Barnstorm's deputies, a shiny brown roach, "looks like we got company, Boss."

"Female company!" announced another of his entourage, face broadly smiling.

CHAPTER 16

"Hi, Barney! Hi there, guys!"

"Mopsy!"

"That's Mopsy Sarsaparilla," whispered an earwig at Bertrand's side, "the mobster's moll. The boys know her as 'Sassy' Sarsaparilla."

"Oh? Why is that, may I enquire?"

"Cos she's real *sassy*, that's why, bub."

"Nothing untoward, I hope."

"Nothing untoward, nope – just *sassy*. Sassy as a grasshopper on a trampoline, the sassiest gal in town."

A good-looking and self-assured ladybird (or lady*bug*, if you like) sauntered directly to the group, stopping before Barnstorm. The mobster boss pulled a face, though his cousin could see that it was not at all serious or threatening. In fact, Barnstorm was soon broadly beaming.

"Well, old gal," he said to the ladybird newcomer, "what's happening? Let me hear it. Sock it to me saucily, as you do."

"It's raining up top, Barney," she responded.

"Aw, that's nothing."

"I mean really *really* raining! A ferocious hard rainstorm

over the whole of New York. It'll mean flooding for certain down here."

"We can handle that," said Barnstorm dismissively. "We got the flood channels open, see."

Mopsy turned to cast a critical eye over what she reckoned to be complete strangers. "Who're the out-of-towners? Leastwise, they sure look like out-of-towners."

"Meet my British cousin Bertrand," beamed Barnstorm, "and his English valet."

"Oh dear, no, he is not my valet," put in Bertrand crossly, "he is my very best friend."

Barnstorm was not entirely convinced but accepted his cousin's words. Turning to the ladybird, he went on, "What else is new, Mopsy, my old gal?"

"I've heard that Ratchett's on the prowl again; he can't get enough victims it seems."

"Yeah, well, we certainly can't handle *him*, that's for dead sure."

'And why not?' considered Bertrand in his fertile mind, beginning to see a glimmer of answers to the enormous problem experienced in what would, in normal circumstances, be a wonderful hideout for this insect population.

He mutely mused over the matter some more, his active beetle brain going into overdrive. And at last, it was settled in his mind, for things soon slotted slippingly and surely into a sound solution.

Bertrand now addressed his cousin in an altogether authoritative tone of voice (much like his old schoolmasterly voice), at once commanding full attention. "You see, Cousin, I may have an idea or two."

"Shoot!"

"I beg your pardon?"

"Tell me, buddy boy. Deal the cards, gimme the lowdown."

Our truly English-bred beetle managed to grasp the meaning of this American rigmarole – rigmarole, ha! – but feared to disclose his plans, at least not fully as yet. It required further thought, with a dash of cunning and devilry. Yes, he would give out the answers soon enough.

"I take it, Cousin, that there are plenty of spiders here in this subterranean city of yours?"

"Yeah, you betcha," answered Barnstorm, a curious look on his face.

"Oh, no!" wailed Wally at once.

"What's with him?" wanted to know Barnstorm.

"I am afraid," began Bertrand, "that my wasp friend here suffers from arachnophobia."

"Holy mackerel! What in insect claws is that?"

"He is afraid of spiders – unless they're very big, like tarantulas. He can tackle tarantulas quite skilfully, fearlessly and efficiently, as he indeed proved strikingly once or twice in the recent past."

Wally whispered to his beetle companion, "But spiders are not insects, are they?"

"I know, I know that, dear soul, they are arachnids."

"So, as I pointed out, they are not insects. Not by a long chalk."

"A long…? Oh, never mind."

"So, what are they doing here? If they are here," pressed Wally.

"There are no prejudices here, one would readily assume. They are all welcome, I would dare to say. At any rate, I find that spiders can sometimes be useful to us insects. As chickens are to human beings."

"Though humans kill and eat chickens, all the time – the savages!"

"Ah yes, well, I simply want to take advantage of the spider's remarkable ability in web-weaving."

Wally smiled a knowing smile. "You're weaving something yourself. You're up to something; I can always tell."

"I am indeed, and, my dear Wallace, you shall know of it in due course."

Bertrand turned to Barnstorm and went on: "These spiders now, Cousin, are they to be trusted? Implicitly?"

"Imp – *impliss* – oh yeah, you bet, brother," said Barnstorm. "For instance, there's Sam Spinner and there's Sid The Sinner. Both good, reliable guys. On my payroll, in fact."

"Can you contact them?"

"Can do, sure as corncake cookies, I can get them on the web."

"The web?"

"Yeah, ya'know, the website. Ain't you got an iPeck?"

"Yes, of course, I see what you mean. It momentarily slipped from my mind."

"Easily done, I guess…" came the American cousin's coarse and somewhat callous response.

"Yes, I do have many matters on my mind," admitted Bertrand, thinking now not of spiders but other possible useful creatures.

CHAPTER 17

Presently, Bertrand approached his cousin with another request. "I shall require the assistance of non-funky, fully functioning slugs, if such exist down here."

"They're on my payroll too. My, oh my!" enthused Barnstorm with delight. "Slugs! This sure is dandy! This caper is gonna be one real swell dilly! Slugs, ha!"

Wally, a little puzzled, whispered to his friend: "Bertie, what is a dandy? What's a dilly? Dandy and dilly, sounds quite silly."

"A sore point, I know, but simply a sample of surplus or studied Americanisms these insects come out with in these parts. One needs to take them with a pinch of pepper."

"Ahh... there is more to this than meets the antennae." And the wasp wandered off.

Meanwhile, Barnstorm was discussing slugs with Stud, one of his beetle minions...

"Who do you reckon then, Stud?"

"There's Harry."

"Harry Lime?"

"No, Harry Slime."

"Yeah, of course! Why didn't I think of that?"

"Ya got much on yer mind, Boss." (Possibly hoping to earn a gold star for this!)

"Yeah, guess so. But hey! Harry Slime and his Sluggers. Great slugs: slimy, sloppy, smelly, real messy. I like it!"

"Sure thing, Boss, that's who you need for dirty work, and Harry's around somewhere near cos I can smell him."

"I'm here, right behind you, Barney," announced a slovenly, slippy, slimy slug.

"Ah, Harry Slime, just the jerk I needs; leastways, my cousin here does. He's the one who needs your help. And by the bye, Harry, where in sewage land have you been? You stink terribly… horribly!"

"Aw, Barney, I was a-courting Sally Slinker down in the sewers," explained the slug a shade shamefacedly.

"So that's why there's one almighty powerful pong around here; ya could cut it like a cheesecake."

"Ah well," began Slime shyly, "you tend to get carried away when you're in love, and my dear Sally, she—"

"Yeah, yeah!" Barnstorm interrupted the other. "Your Sally is a swell dame, no doubt, quite a broad, huh?"

"Quite a slinker, actually."

"Hmm, well, you can *can* that for the present. My cousin here has special instructions for you. Ain't that right, Bertie?"

"Yes, indeed," confirmed Bertrand, "I could certainly do with the specific skills of a slug – several slugs to suit the situation."

Slime and his slug colleagues were almost immediately on the job. Not at all sluggish about it (if you'll forgive the impertinence of putting it that way!), but super-snappy swift.

"Not right now and not here, Slime!" Barnstorm burst

out like a barn-sized bomb. "Later, okay? When an' where my cousin says, got it?"

"Are you sure?" asked a voice deep in slurp and sludge.

"Sure, I'm sure, as sure as sugar-soaked sherbet sticks."

"Okay-dokey, Barney – slime down, fellers!" thrown to his messy, smelly slug team.

"Well, what's ya pitch, Cousin?" enquired Barnstorm with mounting interest. "What're you cooking up, or mebbe I ought not to know, huh?"

"Let this one be a surprise," Bertrand answered him teasingly with a conspiratorial smile, "though certain aspects I can disclose… now, as I see it," continued the ex-schoolmaster beetle, "this is an equation, a mathematical problem, decidedly so. We need to attack this rat menace from at least three sides, as it were, much like a polygon."

"Polly gone?" queried the New York mobster, vastly puzzled.

"I mean a point of many angles, dear soul, not about a parrot gone missing."

"So, is that the lowdown?" asked Barnstorm, impressed despite himself. "The genuine dope, huh? My, what a smart set-up this could be! What a swank showdown and not a let-down. Bertie, old palsy, you're a bona fide smash knockout! I'm impressed, mightily impressed – you catch my drift? It sure sounds a sure cinch, or mebbe could be—"

"Now, there is another particular requirement which perhaps you can assist with…" Bertrand gazed about with keen interest, then went on: "Are there by any chance glow-worms too down here?"

"Glow-worms!"

"On your payroll, no doubt," said with – in human terms, tongue-in-cheek – a half-humoured expression on his face.

"Sure thing, pal, because as it happens, I *do* have a few glow-worms on my payroll. Jeez, ya want the whole caboodle, huh? Anyways, glow-worms I got. They kinda light up my life, ha-ha! You get it? They *light up* my life!"

"Most amusing, I dare to say," returned the other, now with a straight and severe look. "I shall be requiring their services, if it is permissible and not too much trouble."

"None at all, but say, buddy, what exactly are you up to with my worms?"

Bertrand briefly began to explain what he had in mind for his plan of getting rid of the giant rat Ratchett menace, but didn't give his American cousin the essential details.

"It sounds swell, Bertie, you cunning devil you! Sure hope it works. And yeah, my insects and others who live around here will do exactly what I – what you – say, when or where they might be needed."

"Splendid!" smiled Bertrand with satisfaction. "Let us make a start at once."

First of all, he sent Wally to the maintenance cabin he had earlier bounced up against, in order to possibly search out a tin of red phosphorescent paint. This part of his scheme he had kept to himself.

Barnstorm glanced askance at his English beetle kin. *What's he really up to? Some kind of British ingenuity and know-how, I'll bet.*

The mobster would allow the dice to roll 'any which way', as they say in New York City street jargon. Then he changed the subject altogether: "Incidentally, Bert," he opened up in warm, friendly, though somewhat confidential, tones, "we're having a 'smash-an'-grab' tonight, and you're more than welcome to join us."

Bertrand glared back at him with indignation. "Thank

you, Cousin, but no, thank you," he returned primly and disapprovingly. "I have no desire nor inclination to participate in your criminal activities whatsoever ever."

The mobster laughed at this truly English outburst. "No, you got me wrong, buddy boy. When I say *smash*, I mean a *bash*. Ya know, a party with drinks and dancing. And *grab* refers to grabbing grub – or a dancing partner. So, are you game?"

"In that case, I accept your kind invitation with cordial thanks. Could Wallace – Wally, that is – could he also come along? He is my best friend, as you will appreciate."

"Yeah, sure, bring along your will-of-the-wisp."

"Wasp," came the correction.

"That's what I thought I said."

"However, Cousin, before these light entertainments become enlightened, it is imperative that we tackle this Ratchett problem. It is likely that the rat will be on the rampage again before very soon."

"Sure to be, goes without saying. You again, Sassy! What now?" the mobster almost exploded at the ladybird moll who suddenly appeared before him.

"Shall you be going to the ball tonight, Barney? It should prove a real razzle-dazzle affair."

"Nope. Nix to that. After our party, I'll be at the ball *game* on Madison."

"Oh, do go to the ball, Barney, not the ball game. And you can take me with you." Sassy's eyelashes were madly fluttering. "The Coolidge Clan will be clad in their Colin Cline clothes: a red button here and there on their spats, white-spotted black bow tie… and oh! Wait'll you see Frankie McFly look ever so fine in his full-fitting fawn fedora!"

"Jeez! All I need, flighty flirting fairies! Dames!" declared Barnstorm dramatically. "Darned dames! Two a dime, I dare to say; drive ya dotty, they do indeed – gimme a break, Sassy, beat it! Blow!"

"You really mean that, Barney dear?" said a downcast, crestfallen ladybird.

"Sure, I do!" bristled Barnstorm. "Go take a powder. Skedaddle! Scram!"

Sassy soon sailed off, her feelings hurt beyond measure, and the New York mobster unconcernedly and totally indifferently turned to his English guests.

"Before the action, let's go take coffee and cake, chums."

"Coughin' on cake crumbs?" said Wally.

"What's with this wise guy pal of yours?" Barnstorm beetled his brows at the wasp. "Any more wisecracks outa him an' I'll wipe the deck with him!"

Staring now at Bertrand, he continued ranting: "If this limey wasp wants trouble, I can give it to him – I invented trouble."

Bertrand attempted to make a peaceful gesture, smiling pleasantly at his irate American cousin. "Please, you should not mind Wally, his *rascalities* and *misbehaviourals*." He paused a moment. "As for coffee and cake – if I may so express it – I venture to inform you that there is little time for such frivolous civilities."

For Bertrand had decided it was time now to put into execution his plans for finally ridding the giant rat Ratchett from the insect population in this underworld.

CHAPTER 18

The spiders Sam Spinner and Sid The Sinner, along with several of their spider colleagues and friends, were busily weaving strong, thick webs.

"A little higher up, if you would please, you chaps!" advised Bertrand, superintending at ground level.

Sam spun a thread that was singularly taut – tight as a viola string, as he would himself say – and accidently plucked at it. It gave a surprisingly tuneful note.

Mopsy Sarsaparilla, standing and watching nearby, burst into a fit of giggles.

"Did you like that?" grinned Sam, and immediately began spinning more tight threads and playing tunes on them like a true virtuoso.

Barnstorm was about to say something about it, but Wally anticipated him. "I know what you're going to say – 'Play it again, Sam!'."

The New York beetle gave him an unfriendly look. "I was gonna say 'Cut the capering,' that's what I was gonna say, you knuckleheaded limey wasp!"

Later, when they were together, Wally complained to Bertrand. "I don't think your cousin likes me much. I think he has an *altitude*."

"An *altitude*? Ah, you must mean attitude."

"That's what I said."

"No, dear soul," Bertrand pattered out in quick time, "that is only his New York City banter; brusque, brash and businesslike, and no doubt with a face as red as a bishop's bib."

"He said just a minute ago, he said, 'You lookin' at me, you nuthead limey *wusp*!' and I told him I'm a *wasp*, not a *wusp*. And he said I was the *wusp* wasp he'd ever seen!"

"I suppose he meant 'worst wasp'. Moreover, Cousin Barnstorm is – as they say in this most untoward city – the *big-shot* around here. But you are a fine wasp, Wallace; a fine, upstanding, loyal soul, that you are; don't ever forget it."

"Thank you, Bertrand," said the wasp, well satisfied.

Meanwhile, on Bertrand's implicit instructions, Harry Slime and his slug team had left a thick, broad stretch of slime, sludge and slippy slug slurry… directly before the rat's chosen escape route. Chosen route? The giant rodent had no other recourse, Harry later explained, the area hemmed in on two sides like traffic road barriers.

"Do you hear that?"

Everyinsect listened to a great roaring sound, as of a large waterfall. And it was indeed a large fall of water.

Rainwater!

From the city streets and gushing down in torrents to this lower level. Rushing and filling a wide, deep floodwater channel.

"That suits just fine!" smiled Bertrand to himself.

"He's coming!" cried a cockroach voice – it may have been the youngster Ed Crusher.

"*Ratchett's here!*"

"To your stations, everyinsect!" ordered Bertrand with a loud, commanding bellow. "Quickly now!"

The giant rodent came scurrying into view, its long tail lashing out with awful intent.

"*Lights out!*"

CHAPTER 19

It was now a truly and unmistakably subterranean blackworld. This did not trouble the rat so much, as he could still see well enough in the dark. Nonetheless, he was troubled, or at least rendered confused, over the lighting going out.

How and why did that happen? He pressed forward all the same, long, sharp claws scraping on the ground.

Although it was dim and gloomy down here, it was far from quiet. Rainwater dripped and splashed down from street level. This was drowned out – if you will allow the narrator putting it that way – by a constant roar of floodwater rushing into the flash flood channel.

Everyinsect – and Ratchett – also heard a distant clattering, metal-jangling, deep drumming sound that was becoming increasingly louder… and LOUDER!

A subway train was about to cross over on its tracks above them.

Ratchett stopped in *his* tracks, face frozen in fear. For directly ahead of him were many huge pairs of sinister, slantwise, fiery-red eyes! *What manner of monsters are they?* he fearfully wondered. (Only glow-worms painted all over with red phosphorescent paint!)

The rodent Ratchett took several steps back, began skidding and sliding in slimy sludge, slipping sloppily in sticky slug slush.

"*Wally!*"

Wally appeared, buzzing angrily but purposely in the air about the rat. He stung it sharply in one eye, and then again in the other, dead centre of each ratty eyeball.

"Bullseye!" yelled an earwig.

"Ratseye!" another earwig corrected him.

Tears of pain ran down the rodent's raging ratty face, rendering his vision blurry at least.

He turned to make a getaway.

"*Sam! Sid!*"

Down dropped an extensive, thick mass of spiderwebs. Ratchett ran straight into a heavy, tangled mesh of web. He near-blindly threshed about, struggled to free himself. And the more he struggled, the more he became entangled.

Tangled up and tightly tied, he tottered tipsily and toppled into the deep, rushing waters of the finally full-filled flash flood channel. In which was dipped the open, bare wiring of an electric cable. The rat then made a beeline (hope this doesn't offend any insects!) to the cable and made a grab for it in his desperation, as one would grasp for a lifebelt in open waters.

"*Power on!*"

ZING!

The rat's fur frizzled; his body frazzled and fried in a fraction of time.

The subway train, now directly overhead, passed on in a relentless thundering roar!

And Ratchett was dead. Positively, undeniably *dead*!

"*Ratcheted* that one good and proper, eh, Bertie!" smiled Wally happily. "'Dead as a kipper, Skipper!'." (Quoting a famous line of his from a previous story – which you may have already read.)

Ah, Ratchett! His ratty carcass was washed well out into the East River… and total oblivion.

"*Lights on, folks!*"

CHAPTER 20

It is mostly thanks to Sam Spinner
And his spider friend Sid The Sinner
Who set a snare for the rat Ratchett,
Set a super snare to catch it;
So Sid The Sinner is a winner
And his spider friend Sam Spinner.

It was thanks also to the glow-worms, for masquerading as the eyes of giant monsters. A vote of thanks as well to Harry Slime and his far-from-sluggish sluggers! And thanks aplenty go to that brave young wasp Wally for his timely, sprightly stint of striking, his successful stinging spree! It may interest you to know, by the bye, that the mobster's moll Mopsy Sarsaparilla was so grateful that she gave the waspy gallant a hefty smack – of a kiss!

But in the main, all thanks should go to the magnificent planner of a most masterful plan: the brainy, battling, British-born beetle, Bertrand Bartholomew.

"You're quite a fella of action, Bertie Boy," grinned Barnstorm with high satisfaction. "That was a real swell show!"

"A beetle has got to be what a beetle has got to be," smiled Bertrand, at last picking up a fairly appropriate Americanism.

"You did alright too, young stinger," Barnstorm addressed the wasp, with open admiration on his face and a rare kindness in his tone of voice. "There's more to you than meets the eye. Well done, buddy!"

This surprising compliment pleased Wally beyond measure. Finally, and about time too, he was on equal and friendly terms with this tough New York mobster.

Wally and Bertrand found themselves surrounded by happy, grateful insects, busily congratulating the two heroes.

"Stand aside, please! Make way there!" cried a cockroach voice moments later, as someinsect pushed and shoved his way through.

It was Ed. You know him, Ed Crusher.

Bringing in tow a trio of bedraggled waterlogged insect strangers.

"Got them down from the rainstorm still going on up at street level, Boss," explained Ed Crusher. "It's pelting Niagara style up top, fit to put a boat out on it! Oh yeah," he went on with a grin, "these seedpods here are dead certs for out-of-towners," pointing to the three rain-soaked strangers.

Bertrand and Wally could not have been more delighted, and somewhat relieved as well.

"It's Beryl!"

"With Sgt Andy!"

"And Wild Bill!"

"Hi there, Bertrand! Wally!" popped out Beryl.

"Mustered and correctly accounted," announced Sgt Andy in proper military mode.

Spluttered Wild Bill: "I be a rain-rattled storm-stoned wet-watered son-of-a-flood-flashed fool!"

"How in goodness did you find us?" asked Bertrand.

Beryl smiled a sweet smile. "We tracked you on our satpap."

"Don't you mean sat*nav*?"

"No, satpap, it's more accurate and quicker."

"Thank goodness for your iPeck," grinned Wally. "So, how did it go?"

It may be recorded here that these three wet wanderers thoroughly enjoyed – in the words of Wild Bill Hiccup himself – a 'fair-groundin' roller-coastin' dippy-dodgem-dodgin' candyfloss-scoffin' whale-of-a-time at that theer Coney Island fancy frolicsome funfair!'.

CHAPTER 21

A tall, dark, mysterious-looking beetle was seething with frustration. For he had yet to find his most elusive quarry – the Famous Five. The unhappy beetle – we can safely say that this is undoubtedly that travelling menace, Silas Mournmorrow – anyway, he had apparently found a lead. At any rate, he thought he had found a lead. Which at the time miraculously transformed his face from desperate exasperation to one of sweet, blessed relief.

It was a lead derived from a little clue, with which to follow with all due diligence. It took him all the way to Chicago – from New York City.

And back again!

The lead became what is commonly termed a 'lemon'. It was a 'cul-de-sac', in other words a dead-end if ever there was one. A real daft dummy, a duff deal, a dud.

So, Silas Mournmorrow returned to New York.

And followed another lead – a positively genuine hot one this time, he realised with a huge ton of hope on his side, which had him travelling once again to that bustling, windy city of Chicago.

All, it might be stated, at near-bankrupting expense which brought tears to the eyes of this frustrated, bedevilled, nerve-wracked beetle.

Only to find in Chicago that he had barely missed nabbing the elusive five insects.

Just an hour ago, he was reliably informed, those five had caught and boarded and set off on the Great Red Chief *locomotive, heading far south-west to Arizona.*

Missed them by one miserable meanly hour!

He at once fell into a terrific tantrum, kicking out at someinsect's personal luggage.

He would catch up with them, oh yes, he vowed darkly and vehemently, stamping and stomping about in a circle. Especially that particular one of the party. That*beetle!*

However, unfortunately for Silas Mournmorrow, he was hampered and delayed by two railroad police. They saw him deliberately kicking baggage that was certainly not his. They regarded him as a menace and a clear and present danger to the public at large and as a beetle who was decidedly disturbing the peace. They swiftly hauled him off to their local lock-up, to deal with later at their leisure.

"But, gentleinsects! Officers!" he kept pleading. "I beg of you, but I have a train to catch!"

PART TWO

ARIZONA

CHAPTER 22

The *Great Red Chief* locomotive, after its long haul from Chicago, Illinois, puffed and clanged and finally hissed to a halt at the dusty rail depot on the edge of town. The town of Tuxedo in the state of Arizona – cowboy country! – and rather a long way south of Chicago. And an exceedingly long distance from Bertrand's Lower Tinklewigglebottom Wood, or Wally's Much Chipping-In-The-Wold, or Wild Bill's Uddersfield, or Beryl and Sgt Andy's Knocktwice-on-Scrub, all in England of course.

Several creatures stepped from the train onto the clapboard platform of Tuxedo Halt. Mostly local ranchers or townsfolk returning from visits elsewhere, and a few Punchero wives. Except for a bunch of five who stood out like a bunch of red-nosed bananas. Well, four to be honest about it, looking such dudes in their attire, the fifth one at least dressed for the part – Wild Bill no less. They stared around them with amazement and astonishment. What a wonder!

"Wow! This is a *real* Western town!" declared Sgt Andy.

"Could be Dodge City, circa 1888," guessed Bertrand.

"I wonder if Jessicle James is in town?" said Wally.

"What's that lovely smell?" sniffed Beryl with greedy pleasure.

"Bumblebeef dung," grinned Wild Bill. "Sweet, ain't it? This is what ah call *home*. Yippee yahoo!"

A weevil rail porter passed them down their baggage, and they slowly trudged into the town proper, stepping around huge piles of steaming whiffy bumblebeef dung.

At a livery stable, the visitors' attention was taken by a tall, lean cricket cowboy, leaning nonchalantly against the slatted boards of the stable. And, as Wild Bill, with much ivy-green envy, could see – could not possibly fail to see – the cowboy cricket was loaded, far and away absolutely *loaded* with glinting gunmetal gunware!

"Oh, my Aunt Eliza!" bubbled Beryl with a sizzling thrill. "What a tall and lean and handsome-looking cowboy! What a dish!"

The cowpoke smiled charmingly in real Southern fashion on the awe-struck group. He slowly nudged his Stetson up a fraction with equally disarming charm, and just as slowly drawled: "Howdy, folks! Guess you be out-of-towners, huh?"

"Out of the country, actually," Bertrand smiled in return. "We have come all the way from England."

"Well, burn-a-barn-before-breakfast! Wowee! I'm sure surprise-smacked-an'-smothered! Ya don't say!" duly drawled the cowboy.

"I say that!" Wild Bill whispered to Wally with wrath.

"Then yourn be limeys," drawled the cowboy with a grin. "Well, slap-ma-saddle an' cut-a-caper-with-a-coyote, I'll be bandy bug-gone!"

"He's usin' ma lines! He's a-takin' ma lines!" whispered Wild Bill with heat. "He's a-talkin' jist like me!"

"Ya gotta place to hit the hay?" enquired the cowboy in friendly tones.

"We are booked in at the Double Dollar Hotel," explained Bertrand politely. "At least us four males are – the ladybird is to stay at Mrs Grubbub's Boarding House for Young Females, aren't you, Beryl?"

Beryl shyly acknowledged this with a soft murmur, eyeing the tall, lean, handsome cricket cowboy under her long lashes.

"Miss," said the cowboy, touching his Stetson as a mark of respect for the fair sex.

Beryl simply simpered, heart simmering, like a lovelorn maiden.

"Why is everything here so… so *old Wild West*?" wanted to know Sgt Andy, his roving military eye professionally assessing the calibre of the cowboy's gunware.

"Well, stranger," began the other in a dragging drawl, "we aims to keep up our traditions from the past. To maintain an' preserve the past. An' to all intents an' purposes, *live* the past in the present."

The cowboy pushed his Stetson to one side of his head and started to scratch at his scalp. "Ah'm usually a fella of few words," he drawled on, "an' ah nivver talked as much as this since ma schooldays, when ah once had to recite chapter and verse of *The Insect Guide To America*."

Bertrand was eager to change the subject, thinking they could be here all day with this slow-talking local. "Is the Double Dollar Hotel far from here, sir?" he asked with perfect British politeness.

"On Main Street, sir – that's this street, this the only street in town – halfway down on yer left," responded the cowboy pleasantly.

"Is it near Barleybean's Hardware Store at all?"

"Why, yessir, ya hit the butt right in the gut. Barley's opposite the hotel."

"He is my cousin, you see, Barleybean is," said Bertrand with some pride. "In point of fact, that is why we are here, to visit him."

"Yer don't say!" said the cowboy. "Well, danged if I be a surprise-suckered didn't-know-diddled-doddled sorry son-of-a-broadsheet bender!"

"Theer he goes agin!" fiercely whispered Wild Bill at Wally's side. "The copycat critter! The varmint!"

"But he ain't in store for business," continued the cowboy laconically. "Leastwise not right this minute. Gone a-fishin' by Crooked Cricket Creek. Be back by sundown ah guess."

"At least he still lives here, how splendid!" enthused Bertrand with enormous relief. "And thank you, sir, ever so much. We can check in at the hotel and see Barleybean later, I do suppose."

"An' ah'm here to see ma nephew," cut in Wild Bill, addressing the cowboy. "Yer mebbe know him, William Hiccup is the name."

"William?" said the other, a trifle puzzled. "Ah, yeah," he went on at last, losing the puzzled expression. "He used to work as relief bartender at the Double Dollar Saloon."

"Don't he still?" queried Wild Bill, becoming a smattering alarmed.

"No, stranger, he don't," returned the cowboy. "A short while back he took over old Jess Codnapple's tradin' post out of town. Dealin' with Puncheros an' general travellers usually."

"Can ah find this trading place easily enough?" wanted to know Wild Bill.

"Sure, yer jist folla the track heading south out of town. It ain't far." The cowboy paused a moment, as if deliberating on what he ought to say next. Having decided, he came out with it: "Yer know what they call him in this territory, this nephew of yourn?"

"Nope, can't say as I do," admitted Wild Bill.

The cowboy smiled broadly. "They call him 'Willy The Kid.'"

Which certainly put a look of complete and utter surprise on Wild Bill's face.

CHAPTER 23

"Tell me, mister," went on Wild Bill, a smidgen aggressively at the cowboy cricket, "Yer reckon this is a lawless kinda town?"

The local eyed him up and down with faint amusement and replied: "No more than usual in this 'ere territory. There was a while back the gunfight at the Okey Kokey Corral. Nuthin' much doin' since then, ah do declare."

"Sorted by Wyatt Twerp, I guess, huh?"

"Nope."

"Skipalong Cassidy?"

"Nope."

"Davy Cluckett?"

"No, sirree."

"Who then, durn it?"

"Ma own self!"

"Oh, how exciting!" gushed Beryl, still gaping at the tall, lean handsome cowboy. She thought of him as most *eyeable*, like a film star.

"No Punchero trouble around these parts?" pursued Wild Bill.

"Sometimes… some times…" mused the cowboy in quiet tones. "There's a local tribe, the Woppapache Puncheros, but they're kinda tied down on their reservation, which ain't too far from here, by the bye."

"Do they come out a-raidin' at all?" pushed Wild Bill.

"They do that once in a while, yessir," said the other.

"Are they fierce kind of warriors?" enquired Sgt Andy.

"Sure, when they gets riled," came the response.

"How do they get riled, as you put it?" asked Bertrand.

"Well, the Woppapache are tied to the reservation, as ah said," began the cowboy, "but they get an urge at times to go out and hunt bumbleuffalo, which ain't allowed now by State law."

"*Bumbleuffalo*?" burst from Beryl. "What are *bumbleuffalo*?" turning to Sgt Andy for enlightenment.

"Great shaggy hairy beasts, my pet," said the soldier ant, "that freely roam the plains. The Puncheros have hunted bumbleuffalo since time out of mind."

"Whatever for?"

"Their meat to eat, pet, hides for clothing and to make wigwams. Bumbleuffalo is essential to the Woppapache Punchero culture. Shame they have to be holed up on a miserable reservation. It's not natural for them."

"Don't ever get yourselves captured by the Woppapache," warned the cowboy, "or yer in real sticky treacle."

"How's that?" said Wild Bill, slightly intrigued.

"They torture their victims… by ticklin' them to death."

"Oh, how horrible!" exclaimed Beryl, appalled at such wanton cruelty.

"Well, we must get on," voiced Bertrand decidedly. "Thank you most kindly for your time, sir," smiling gratefully at the cowboy. "So, it is straight on for the Double Dollar establishment, but Mrs Grubbub's Boarding House, where would that be, we all wonder?"

"Yes," put in Beryl, "I wish to retire and rest as soon as possible, after our long, weary travelling," looking up helplessly at the tall, lean, handsome one.

"Why, miss," he drawled, touching his Stetson in courtly fashion, "allow me to escort you. Ah'll take yer right to the boarding house porch – is this yore bag? If that's okay, sir?" turning to Bertrand for permission.

"Yes, certainly, by all means," flustered Bertrand, also captivated by the easy Southern charm of this strikingly handsome cowboy, "er… Mister…?"

"Eatwood's the name, folks," drawled the cowboy with a fetching smile, "Squint Eatwood."

CHAPTER 24

A short while later found our travel-worn male guests at their ease in the Double Dollar Hotel saloon, knocking back slugs of potent slug juice – the 'real McCoy' as Wild Bill phrased it with high pleasure.

A few slugs on and the town's sheriff, a broad-backed basalt-black beetle, sauntered in and casually parked himself at their table. He was eager to know a little more about these Englishsect visitors.

Sheriff Fiddlebucket was indeed a hefty, solid specimen, twice as broad in the back as Wild Bill, with a hard and threatening 'You lookin' at me?' expression on his face. All the same, as the others appreciated, he was pleasant enough, sensing rightly that he need not fear any kind of disorderly conduct from these four mild-mannered insects from England – not even the dude trying to make out to be a Wild Bill Hickok.

"Yessirs, Tuxedo is one mighty fine *quiet an' peaceful* town at the present," Sheriff Fiddlebucket was informing the visitors in complacent, though firm, tones, "and ah aim to keep it that way."

He glanced meaningfully over at Wild Bill, who was absently stroking the butt of his Bolt 45, and went on. "Yessirs, ah'm due retirement pretty soon an' ah don't aim to tolerate any trouble in town. No, sirs, not in *my* town. Leastways, not till ah slings in my badge of office come retirement time."

"What will you do, Sheriff, once you are retired?" politely enquired Bertrand. He kept glancing around the room, wondering how much longer his cousin Barleybean was going to be out fishing.

"Ah aims to open up a fancy gambling saloon," said Sheriff Fiddlebucket. "Not like this tin-pot run-down no-good corn-shack!"

He eventually prepared to take his leave of them, with some homely parting words: "Guess we'll meet up agin, fellas, by an' bye, so it's bye for now, goodbye!"

And he sauntered from the premises.

CHAPTER 25

It could not have been but an eye blink or a cat wink later when the saloon doors crashed open and in rushed a harassed-looking jewel beetle. He held a fishing rod and a basket. So, it couldn't have been anyinsect else but Bertrand's American cousin Barleybean.

Barleybean had apparently enjoyed a successful fishing expedition, for in the basket lay his magnificent catch of three fine tiddlers! He had no further interest in fish or fishing, however, because he dropped the rod and basket by a spittoon and pelted over to the bar counter.

"Jake!" he cried to the bartender, quite flustered or flummoxed or something like as much. "Have you seen the sheriff? He's not in his office, I've just come from there, and I have simply got to see the sheriff!"

"He left here only in a shake of a rattler's rattle," the bartender told him. "Prob'ly doin' his rounds. Why, Barleybean, what's happened?"

"Hello, Barleybean," put in Bertrand softly, such joy catching at his thorax as he tapped his cousin on the back.

Barleybean swung round and came face to face with his English cousin. The beetles were alike as two front teeth – black teeth of course.

"Bertrand?"

"The same, dear cousin," smiled Bertrand happily.

"Well, slap me silly, if this ain't the fat end of the wedge! You could knock me over with a feather duster, yessiree!"

"Whatever has happened to your Tinklewigglebottom accent?" said Bertrand. "It has quite disappeared, dear cousin, if I may so say."

Barleybean collected himself together, still flustered or flummoxed or something like, and went on: "Look'ee, Bertrand, we can talk 'family stuff' some other time. Ah've gotta find me a sheriff. Ah'll check you later, Cousin!"

He was about to shoot off but was checked himself when Jake the bartender called over from his counter: "What's goin' on, Barleybean?"

"The Woppapache Puncheros are out and raidin'!" cried the hardware storekeeper. "They nabbed Willy The Kid from the trading post!"

"Why'd they snatch little Willy?" pursued Jake.

"He sold 'em some manky bumbleuffalo robes, by all accounts, an' now the critter's forrit!"

With that, Barleybean was through the saloon doors, fishing tackle quite abandoned and forgotten.

CHAPTER 26

"*This* calls fer action!" gruffed Wild Bill belligerently.

"*This* means war!" declared Serge**ant** Andy with an equal force of belligerence.

"*This* is real exciting stuff!" mouthed Wally a little foolishly.

"*This* requires a plan," said Bertrand practically.

A plan? What sort of a plan? A good workable plan? Yes, why not? reasoned Bertrand to himself. They may live in the past here in Tuxedo, Arizona, but the Englishsect visitors had brought with them certain resources of the modern technological world.

Namely, each had in his possession a hi-tech iPeck; yes, an iPeck, one of the latest wonders of insect communication technology, and far superior to the earlier iPud models. *These tools could prove extremely useful,* vouched Bertrand… to himself.

"Here is how we go about it, my friends," opened up the brain-brimmed beetle, "and we can forget about getting help from the sheriff, or any posse he might muster, and all that historical woolly Wild West doolally. Listen now! As these Woppapache Puncheros are apparently at times desperate to hunt the so-called bumbleuffalo but are not allowed off their reservation, well, we can take advantage of that fact."

"How?" asked Sgt Andy.

"How!" said Wally in his silly mode. "Me wantum hunt prairie bumbleuffalo!"

"Stow it, Wally, yer cactus pip!" growled Wild Bill.

"Yes, affirmative," put in the soldier ant, "let us be a bit more orderly and commonsensible about this."

"Firstly," continued Bertrand, "to imitate the sound of a prairie bumbleuffalo – can anyinsect do that?"

"I can!" volunteered Wally, quick off the mark here, "just listen to this… *OOT! OOT!*"

"That is remarkable! Perfect!" enthused Bertrand. "Wally, you sounded exactly like a bumbleuffalo. In fact, more like a herd of bumbleuffalo. It was uncanny."

"I can also do the mating call of a chuckle-paddle bug."

"That will not be necessary at this moment in time," said Bertrand with a deal of severity in his voice.

"So, what then?" wanted to know Sgt Andy.

"A simple procedure actually," declared Bertrand with enormous satisfaction. "We record the sound of bumbleuffalo on our iPecks, upload to maximum amplifier mode and play back very loud and clear!"

"For what purpose?" Sgt Andy needed to know.

"We each go with our own personal iPeck," Bertrand began to expand further, "we each go to a far corner of the territory, keeping in constant touch of course, with our trusty iPecks. One plays back the sound of bumbleuffalos, luring the Woppapache from their reservation, thinking it is the real thing – a herd of them!"

"Then when they arrive at the source of the sound," carried on Sgt Andy, catching on immediately to the tactical implications, "it's suddenly switched off…"

"…And another sounds up from another distant corner of the land," continued Bertrand, broadly smiling. "Keep it on like so, making our sounds from every corner of this Wild West…"

"…Until eventually, if matters work out as envisaged, we will have worn the Woppapache down to a helpless exhausted frazzle!"

CHAPTER 27

"I can't wait to see that wee nephew of mine," said Wild Bill with fine filial feeling.

Said Wally: "I can't hardly wait to *OOT! OOT!*"

And the plan, as Bertrand had so confidently foreseen, worked a treat and without a hitch, when they later surveyed a sorry scene before them.

The entire male tribe of Woppapache warriors lay prostrate on the ground, near to the entrance of what is locally known as Gigglestone Gulch. The Woppapache Puncheros were positively pooped and frazzled to a turn, and certainly in no condition to do anything other than sleep off their total exhaustion.

"We can get on now to the reservation," said Bertrand, "and pick up poor little Willy."

"What about the Punchero wives?" said Sgt Andy.

"The Punchero wives won't give us any trouble whatsoever ever, if I may so say," replied Bertrand firmly.

"I wouldn't count on it," warned Wally. "They can be nasty, them Punchero wives. I'll bet they're torturing Willy right this minute."

"If they are at all any bother to us, my dear Wallace,"

countered his friend, "I intend to set *you* on them."

"That's setting the cat among the pigeons!" laughed Sgt Andy.

"But what about my little Willy?" moaned Wild Bill. "What if they've eaten the wee feller?"

"No, Billy," pattered in Sgt Andy, "as that Squint Eatwood chap in Tuxedo told us, the Woppapache torture their victims by tickling them to death."

"Of course! Of course!" exclaimed Wild Bill jubilantly. "That's alright then!"

"Alright! Why's that?" chorused the others.

"Because…" said Wild Bill with a wink and a smirk, "because our little Willy ain't ticklish!"

As the four friends neared the site of the Punchero reservation, Bertrand fell in at the rear alongside of Wally.

"Just look at Billy Hiccup," commented Bertrand, "isn't he so like your typical cricket!"

"Yes," agreed Wally, "I was thinking the same. He reminds me of a thin stick."

"Wassat?" barked Wild Bill, quickly turning round and sensing something amiss.

"We were just saying, Billy," offered Wally glibly, "how you've put on a bit of weight in your middle age."

"Put on a bit o' weight, huh?" gruffed Wild Bill, not entirely feeling offended but perhaps proud of this supposed condition. "I guess yore right at that. I'm what you'd call a broad-butted beer-barrelled bulge-bellied son-of-a-sumo-wrestler!"

Moreover, and pleasant to relate, a happy, joyful cricket indeed was Wild Bill, after business on the Punchero reservation was swiftly and effectively dealt with.

Wild Bill was at last reunited with his young nephew, known colloquially and locally as Willy The Kid.

CHAPTER 28

Much awhile later (about as much, Good Reader, as it takes to shift a duffbug-burger, a whole corn-on-the-cobble, and a rhubarb salad with nut-nobs); yes, much awhile later in the town of Tuxedo, Sheriff Fiddlebucket was congratulating the Englishsect visitors on their remarkable action with the Woppapache hostiles.

"Yessirs! You fellers sure put paid to them pesky Puncheros, with them clever contraptions of yourn – them *iPucks* as yer call 'em."

"It is **iPeck**, Sheriff," corrected Bertrand. "An upgrade from the old iPud."

"Well, whatever ever, yer did mighty fine all the same, an' ah thank'ee mightily."

No sooner had the Sheriff uttered this (about as long as it takes to wolf down and demolish a choccy chuckle chip cookie), when there happened a sudden commotion further up the main street of this Western township.

"Outlaws!" cried a caterpillar cowboy. "An' they jist vamoosed right outta town!"

"Outlaws, yer say?" spluttered the outraged law-insect.

"That's right, Sheriff," returned the caterpillar cowpoke. "They done burst into Mrs Grubbub's boarding house—"

"They done what!" stormed the Sheriff in a fury.

"And abby-abby-abducted one of the females. The limey ladybug, I believe."

"Oh my Aunt Minnie!" burst from Bertrand. "Some devilish rascals have taken our Beryl hostage!"

"A rout! This is disastrous! A defeat!" shot out Serge**ant** Andy.

"This is a downright imp-imp-impudence!" declared Wally hotly.

"I'll shoot out their eyeballs!" threatened Wild Bill. "The varmints!"

"Is it the James Gang?" asked Sheriff Fiddlebucket.

"No, it ain't them, Sheriff," responded the caterpillar. "There're only two of 'em."

"Just two, huh?" the Sheriff grinned wickedly. "We'll soon sort out two liddle lawbreakers."

"All very well yer sayin' that, Sheriff," continued the caterpillar cautiously, "but I ain't yet told yer their names."

"Names is nuthin," the Sheriff replied dismissively. "But who are these two characters anyway?"

The caterpillar cowboy had no intention of panicking the populace. He sidled up to Sheriff Fiddlebucket, and at his side whispered:

"*Budge Cassidy and The Tapdance kid*!"

Crickets of a chronic cruel kind…

CHAPTER 29

While Tuxedo's Sheriff hastily rustled up a posse, Bertrand asked the caterpillar cowpoke what transpired at Mrs Grubbub's boarding house, and what might she had to say about this calamitous affair.

Mrs Grubbub explained how two desperados had forced their way in through the front parlour of her respectable establishment, and boldly entered the sacred and private ladies' lounge.

"Pick the prettiest!" apparently growled one outlaw, most likely Budge Cassidy, "an' let's high-tail it outta here!"

His accomplice, The Tapdance Kid, clapped eager roving eyes over the frightened, cowering crowd of young females. And immediately made his choice.

He had of course chosen Beryl.

The poor ladybird was scooped up, thrown roughly over Tapdance's shoulder.

He then tripped, tapped, and tango'd right out of the house.

Budge Cassidy was close behind him.

CHAPTER 30

"We should never have brought Beryl to this wild lawless place," complained Sgt Andy bitterly.

"It ain't that wild," countered Wild Bill. "Now Uddersfield was wild. *Was*, mind yer, till ah stomped a kronker on their reckless shenanigans."

"I sure hope Beryl is carrying her hi-tec iPeck," said Bertrand with concern. "I have a strong feeling that it may come in handy fairly soon."

"She is! She has got it alright!" cried Sgt Andy, picking at his own iPeck. "I'm tracking her now on the *SatNav Eyeball*."

"Splendid!" said Bertrand with evident relief and satisfaction. "Now all it requires is another simple and effective plan."

"Yer got one?" asked Wild Bill.

"Yes, any good ideas?" said Sgt Andy, keen to soldier on and make some grand strategic movement of manoeuvre.

"Possibly…" answered Bertrand. "Hmm. Probably." He went on with rising voice and hope: "Oh, yes… certainly as I see the matter materialising. Positively in fact!" as ideas tumbled and stormed inside his fertile insect think-tank.

"Good show!" was Sgt Andy's comment.

"Now we'll top them!" grinned Wally. "Top and tail them!"

"We'll sure lick 'em!" Wild Bill afire with anticipation and downright derring-do.

"In the meantime," continued Bertrand, showing a decided clip and snap to his demeanour. "In the meantime, fellows, let us join the Sheriff and his posse. And, if you pay due attention, I'll tell you a little about my plan…"

STABLES

CHAPTER 31

A tall dark black-hatted stranger stepped from the train in which he had spent many long and weary travelling hours. He alighted with a lightness of heart and a spring to his step, a most unusual state for him to be in, it might be added.

For this was Silas Mournmorrow.

He found himself in an empty, desolate and deathly quiet place. However, this was not of any consequence to him, and nor would it alter his rare good mood – at least for the present. It would seem to him that this very day would at last see the culmination of his exhaustive travels and sordid searching.

So this is Tuxedo, Arizona, he thought happily. Not at all what he had imagined, not at all a pleasant place, no distinction, no style; in short, a proper dump! But never mind, for that is of no particular account or even interest – as he looked about with distaste at the most miserable surrounds he had ever encountered. Dust and cobwebs covered lowly slatted wooden shacks in dilapidated, neglected condition. Tumbleweed rolled along an empty main street, the only street in fact of this lonely and seemingly deserted town. There was noinsect anywhere in sight, he concluded.

"Can I help yer, mister?"

The voice, coming from behind him and coming so suddenly, so unexpectedly, that it made him jump with fright.

"Oh, hello there! I never expected Tuxedo Town to look like this," said Silas Mournmorrow by way of response, addressing a small dust-covered beetle railroad worker, going by his uniform.

"Mebbe because," drawled the little beetle, "this 'ere ain't Tuxedo Town."

Silas Mournmorrow stared at the insect aghast. "This is Tuxedo? The town of Tuxedo, Arizona?" he managed to splutter.

The railroad insect eyed the stranger with a mixture of contempt and amusement – 'What a tall black streak of nothing!' he must have thought – "At the last halt, Roughhide Junction," he began to explain, "yer should have changed trains to get to Tuxedo."

"But the porter on my train did not tell me anything about that."

"Porters ain't fer explaining things, mister," retorted the railroad employee. "Yer need an information clerk fer explaining things."

"So where am I?"

"Yer don't know where you're at?"

"I'm afraid not," admitted Silas Mournmorrow mournfully, unmistakably becoming his usual miserable self again – that is to say, decidedly morose, definitely mournful, defiantly mouldy and grim, with a face like he'd eaten a sour plum.

"Well, mister, this 'ere is Tequila, State of New Mexico, fer what it's worth."

"New Mexico! Tequila!"

"Yep, right first time," and the beetle spat in the dust for emphasis and with high satisfaction.

Not having spoken to a living soul in an age, this lone railroad worker went on like a gramophone record with scratched grooves:

"This 'ere's a ghost town, mister, an' haunted to the hilt – leastwise I expect so, an' if it ain't then it sure ought to be! Noinsect has lived here in nigh a 'undred seasons, mebbe more. Town died when the bumbleuffalo stopped their seasonal run through this 'ere territory. No sirree, no bumbleuffalo, no hides to skin an' sell. The town died a death, all done in and dusted down fer good. A bit like Old Tucson, if yer ask me."

"But my train stopped here!" whined the voice of the long-distance traveller.

"Sure it did. To take on water. That's all."

"And you – you live here?"

"Not as I can 'elp it. Jist come up to fix the waterin' an' mebbe stay awhiles."

"So, you are the..."

"Yep, a water-beetle. That's me!"

"But you don't reside here?"

"Not full time, if I can 'elp it. No, ah jumps into my ole jalopy an' head south fer El Paso. T'ain't far to ole El Paso."

"When is the next train?" enquired Silas Mournmorrow, with merely a thimbleful of hope.

"The Prairie Scout *is about due in two hours I guess."*

"Ah, splendid! That is wonderful! Oh thank goodness!"

"Headin' north fer Las Cruces."

"Oh dear, no!"

Silas Mournmorrow thought a moment, then said, "And the next train west?"

"To Roughhide Junction?"

"Yes, that is it."

"An' change an' on to Tuxedo?"

"Yes, yes!" desperation creeping into the other's voice.

"Tuxedo, Arizona?"

"Of course, Tuxedo, Arizona! Where else, for goodness sake!"

"Well, there 'appens to be a Tuxedo in Texas too. Two Tuxedos! So Tuxedo, Arizona it is, eh?"

"That is correct," returned a voice of pure exasperation.

The little dusty railroad worker collected his dusty thoughts.

"Ain't nuthin' headin' west till a week on Tuesday. Now, lemme see, today is Thursday, so – Hey! Where're yer goin', mister?"

And the railworker beetle, who, because of his particular situation, worked alone for long hours every day, without comfort and without companionship, starved of company and leisure of any kind… This little lonely soul sat himself down to watch for free – and with the same degree of contempt and amusement he had held heretofore…

"Oh my! Oh my! Hot diggerty durn!" he chortled happily, "Ah nivver had so much furn*!"*

… Watched the enterprising antics and foolery of this tall dark streak of a stranger hopping madly about, ranting and raving and raging… kicking down doors of empty clapboard shacks, and vandalising windows, shutters, pathways and posts with positive and wicked intent.

The tall crazy one also indulged in screaming out the most highly colourful language the water-beetle had ever heard in his entire existence!

CHAPTER 32

Sheriff Fiddlebucket's posse tracked the trail of the two bandits to the town of Tostado, sat smack on the border with Mexico.

"Tostado!" cried someinsect in the posse. "They're riding straight into Tostado!"

"Yep!" acknowledged Sheriff Fiddlebucket, "and ah can fully guess why. Only heard the news meself last week."

"What news is that, Sheriff?" asked another of the posse.

"Why, a large haul of gold was deposited in the Tostado Bank fer safekeeping."

"So, it's the gold them varmints are after," gruffed Wild Bill. "They're plannin' on robbin' the bank, huh?"

"It would appear so," said the Sheriff.

"But it *don't* appear so!" cried someinsect else in the posse. "They've ridden *past* the bank, and look'ee, actually headin' fer – well darn me an' darn me socks! – They're headin' fer the Sheriff's Office!"

"They must have some kind of tactical plan," threw in Serge**ant** Andy. "Some kind of *ruse*, I'm *sure*." *

(* Curious, isn't it, that the letters making the word *'ruse'* also form the word *'sure'* – just a passing observation; do please carry on.)

"Ride on, boys!" commanded Sheriff Fiddlebucket.

"Where to, Sheriff?" asked some weak-witted weevil.

"'Where to?' he says," growled the law-keeper with heavy sarcasm. "To Tostado Town, you overripe tomato! You tired tasteless taco! We'll surround them in town, cut off their escape. Ride on!"

Bertrand and Wally, along with Sgt Andy and Wild Bill, all four friends followed freely behind the posse.

CHAPTER 33

Budge Cassidy and The Tapdance Kid were experienced outlaws, wily and cunning, and competent gunfighters. Their own plan was indeed to rob the bank of Tostado and make a getaway by crossing over the border into Mexico, out of reach of any U.S. law-enforcer. They knew of the gold shipment of course, and they wanted that gold really bad, so as to live a life of luxury somewhere in South America.

But first, in order to succeed in their plan it was necessary that the local sheriff be kept occupied, while they emptied the bank of its gold. Which was the reason why they had snaffled the hapless ladybird Beryl.

She was to be used as a kind of decoy, a sort of distraction, to lure the local sheriff a long ways from the bank. To set him up as a sap – as they say in America.

Beryl was to beguile the sheriff with her feminine charms, and keep him out of the way in his own office. If she did not cooperate and do exactly as they wanted, the desperate duo would assuredly rip off her wings, or some such awful punishment.

And such was their dreadful diabolical plan…

CHAPTER 34

It would appear, as things began to turn out, that the robbing rascal duo's dirty plan could possibly fly out the window. For when Beryl entered the sheriff's office in Tostado she was confronted by a…

FEMALE SHERIFF!

And Miss Winifred Leadbiter
Was no mere bedbug-biter;
A long, lifelongish spinster
With a face like York Minster:
All granite and grit
And growl and spit;
The hardiest law-keeper in the West
Doing what she does and doing it the best –
Maintaining strict straight law and order
In this township by the Mexican border.

"Yeah, how can I help you?" she tackled Beryl in testy tones.

"Er… please, ma'am – Sheriff, should I say," blustered Beryl blushingly, "but there are two bandits about to break your bank."

"Is that so! Are they there now?" demanded to know Sheriff Leadbiter, strapping on her gun-belt.

"On their way, ma'am – Sheriff," said Beryl, "as soon as I signal an all-clear. They're waiting outside in the street, mounted on bumblesteeds."

"Well now, let's go take a quick look see," decided Sheriff Leadbiter, and immediately made for the door.

As ill fortune would have it, the moment the female sheriff opened the door, Budge Cassidy, out of nowhere it seemed, made his move and hit her head hard with his gun and she fell to the floor in a flop, quite senseless and totally out of action.

Beryl was snatched up once again, held firm by the strong grip of The Tapdance kid.

The bandit rogues mounted up, Beryl helpless in Tapdance's iron grip. They rode off at once, kicking up a spume of dust.

Only a moment before they had caught sight of the pursuing posse.

CHAPTER 35

The posse soon arrived in the dusty border town of Tostado. Townsfolk began running towards them, all pointing in one direction.

"At the end of town there, Sheriff!" called up one of them, an earwig blacksmith. "They're hiding in the schoolhouse!"

"The schoolhouse!" echoed Sheriff Fiddlebucket in some alarm. "Any kids in there, mister?"

"Sure thing, of course," replied the earwig smithy, "all the kids in town, thirty-two and a half of 'em."

"A half? What do you mean?" queried the Sheriff.

"One's real small, Tiny Tom, and he's a bit crippled too, lost two or three legs. And there's the schoolteacher, Miss Lucy Ladybug – Oh, and another ladybug, who came with the outlaws."

Sheriff Fiddlebucket turned to Bertrand, knowing he had formulated some kind of a plan.

"It is somewhat as I imagined, Sheriff," the British beetle told him.

Bertrand then cast a significant glance at his friends, Wally, Sgt Andy and Wild Bill, and said:

"I'll call Beryl now…"

CHAPTER 36

In the classroom some thirty-odd young ones of all ages – beetles and ants and earwigs, wasps and bees and caterpillars – and two adult ladybirds, were huddled in a mass in one corner. Half frightened out of their wits and fearing for their very lives, the youngsters moaned and whimpered among themselves.

Beryl suddenly caught a *pat-tap* issuing from her iPeck. She glanced nervously over at the two bandits standing at a window, with guns drawn. They appeared too preoccupied in looking out. Beryl cautiously, almost cunningly (certainly surreptitiously, if you can tolerate a longer word!) put the iPeck close to her side.

"Yes?" she whispered, with a catch in her thorax.

"Beryl?" came the familiar voice.

"Oh Bertrand! Oh thank goodness!" breathed Beryl, relief flooding her whole being.

"Are you okay? Are the little ones alright?"

"Yes, Bertrand. We're all in one corner opposite the window – the only window that looks out onto the street."

"Fine! Now listen my dear and listen very carefully. This is what you must do..."

"I'm listening, Bertrand," responded Beryl, her strength of mind and will getting stronger with every growing moment.

"... And amplify to absolute maximum without fail," urged Bertrand, concluding his most specific instructions.

Every young one and the schoolmistress Lucy Ladybug stared expectantly at this ladybird stranger.

"Now children, pay close attention to what I am going to say," began Beryl.

This typical English ladybird of good stock, felt of a sudden somehow matronly, even a little brave. Beryl sensed that she was at last coming into her own as an independent and responsible individual, gaining great power within herself.

Beryl at that crucial moment felt positively **proud** to be British!

"...And it is essential that you all block your antennae as well for your own safety," she finished telling them, "as soon as I give the signal for us all to begin..."

CHAPTER 37

"I'm goin' in there!" declared a member of the posse. It was the tall lean handsome cowboy cricket, Squint Eatwood.

"Hold back on yore reins, yer young hothead!" shot back Sheriff Fiddlebucket fiercely. "You ain't goin' nowhere except on my say-so. Now jus' simmer down, yer young sproggle!"

He turned to view the schoolhouse window, spotting two shadowy figures, and shouted over: "Drop yore guns an' come on out, Budge! You too, Tapdance, nice an' peaceful like. We got yer covered an' surrounded. If you don't make a move, we'll blast yer out!"

"Fire at will, why don't you, Sheriff!" yelled back Budge in tormenting tones, and not intending to *budge* an inch. "We got a whole bunch of kids in here. So you go right ahead and try shooting us out – Ha! Ha!"

"Why, it's a Mexican Stand-Off!" cried Wild Bill. "Danged if I'll be an over-shot ace-deuced double-crossed son-of-a-cross-eyed croupier!"

"Right, chaps!" roared Bertrand in a loud commanding

voice, addressing the posse, "block antennae as I earlier warned. For now is the time!"

He clicked on his iPeck, and spoke three words only:

"Okay, Beryl, NOW!"

CHAPTER 38

There came one great almighty unearthly antennae-slicing

SCREEEECH!

streaming from out the schoolhouse with a massive shock-wave of high-pitched sound.

Every single window in Tostado instantly shattered; every china pot, dish and plate cracked and broke. Cats went berserk, voicing their own catty screech, and bumblesteeds reared up on their hindquarters in fear and fright.

Unable to tolerate the intensity of the terrible drawn-out scream – thirty-and-some youngsters full-throatedly giving it their all, amplified and magnified to towering proportions on Beryl's iPeck – the two bandits soon came rushing out through the door.

Budge Cassidy and The Tapdance Kid came belting out with all guns blazing.

And there this chapter ends.

With the gun-slinging duo frozen in mid-air, as it were, their guns still smoking. As shot upon shot of hot lethal lead came bulleting towards their mortal vitals.

A **dead** reckoning.

SCREECH!

CHAPTER 39

A few days after the events just narrated Sheriff Fiddlebucket spoke pleasantly to the Englishsect visitors:

"By the bye, tonight the township's holding a barn-dance and kinda shake-down by Shakewell livery stable. Should prove a real stomper," he informed them expansively, "an' you're right welcome to join in with the festivities."

"Oh, how splendid!" smiled Bertrand. "We shall be honoured to attend, Sheriff, I am sure."

"Do yer like music, barn-dance style?"

"Not that we know of, however, it no doubt has its merits, I do suppose," admitted the British beetle. "My friend Wallace here is by all accounts an accomplished *buffoonist*."

"Yes," agreed Wally with a grin, "I always play the buffoon."

"Ah can well believe it," the sheriff shot back.

"I really meant to say," confessed Bertrand, red-faced with acute embarrassment, "I meant to say *bassoonist*."

"Ah reckon yer were right first time," pot-shot the sheriff with warm dry humour. "Yep, this here barn-dance caper should prove a right rollicking belly tickler," he went on with a chuckle, "what with our Famous Fancy-Free Fourstep—"

"Nancy-Lee on me doorstep, yer say?" butted in an old-timer.

"No, you deaf old coot!" retorted the Sheriff, quick temper rising. "Ah didn't say Nancy-Lee on yer doorstep, I said the Fancy-Free Fourstep."

"Hee-hee! Ah'm all forrit!" croaked the old-timer. "But wait on, pardner, while ah goes an' slips into me dancing slippers!"

"Daft old duffer!" murmured the Sheriff under his breath. "Silly old crock!"

"Er... hum!"

Someinsect else barging in on the company.

The Sheriff turned to find a dapper looking earwig in a neat natty outfit, standing neat and tidy before him.

"Who the blazes are you!" he blazed at him like a backfiring blowtorch.

"Good day to you, Sheriff! Dapper Doomore's the name, of Do-It-Double Glazing," said the earwig neatly by way of introduction.

"Yep, an' what do yer want?" grizzled the Sheriff bad-temperedly.

"Well, as I understand it, sir," replied the neat dapper earwig in neat clipped precise tones, "I believe you have a few windows in your town that need replacing..."

CHAPTER 40

It was extraordinary how later events played out their course.

If, Dear Reader, you happen to be of a romantic bent of mind, you might possibly have guessed that the ladybird Beryl would eventually marry the tall lean handsome cowboy cricket, Squint Eatwood. He was deemed so good-looking and possessed such winning charm, that his new and devoted wife persuaded him to go into the movie business. Beryl became Squint's public relations representative – and his private secretary as well. They set up home and lived happily in the grand and glorious environs of Wollyhood, California.

It was of course a foregone conclusion as Serge**ant** Andy saw it, and wished the couple well. The veteran soldier-ant also left the group and headed south into Mexico. To visit certain war grave sites, and to pay his respects to fallen comrades in the Mexican Campaigns of '02 – or was it '03?

Wild Bill Hiccup, ever ready to seize an opportunity, volunteered to deputize for Sheriff Fiddlebucket. At the same time Wild Bill made application for Arizona citizenship. And when Fiddlebucket finally fell into retirement – to run his fancy gambling saloon – Wild Bill took over as Sheriff of Tuxedo. He was the perfect one for the job.

His nephew Willy The Kid was taken on as his deputy.

"An' from now on, young 'un," gruffed Wild Bill, "You'll toe the line and behave as a decent insect – or else answer to me… yore trigger-trippin' sure-shootin' slang-slingin' – Uncle!"

That leaves two. Bertrand and Wally. A different story altogether.

"Wallace Warrington Wasp, there is a positive gleam in your eye. You are evidently up to something or other – I can always tell, you know! – Now, dear soul and old friend, what are you thinking of? What are you cooking up in that waspish mind?"

"Well…" Wally hesitated.

"Yes, yes, spit it out."

"Well, I was just thinking, Bertie, here we are in the great American Southwest."

"Yes, in course I am sorely aware of that rock solid fact. Now don't fumble and faffle and do please go on."

"Maybe we could go visit someplace else."

"What someplace else?"

"A pleasant place, a place of interest."

"That sounds pleasant and interesting enough, and not to say also appealing."

"A notable place. A famous place."

"Not that terrible Tombstone town! I have no desire to see the graves of past villains and desperados, or cemetery of any description whatsoever ever."

"No, of course not. I mean a place that's alive and active, a place of excitement and thrills."

"If I may so say that indeed sounds like a place worth visiting…"

Bertrand ruminated and pondered and mused. "Hmm…"

Wally had him netted!

"Oh it is, Bertie, I do believe, well worth a visit. It is, no word of a lie. Honest."

"Very well, I shall take your word for it. Might I ask, what exact place is it you speak of so highly?"

Wally took a deep breath. Then plunged in.

"LAS VEGAS!"

MOTEL
MGM
Fabulous
LAS VEGAS
NEVADA

CHAPTER 41

Silas Mournmorrow was in Las Vegas, in the desert State of Nevada. How such a morose and miserable individual could be in such a fun-loving town as Las Vegas would normally be beyond belief. All the same, he was here for a specific purpose. A reliable tip-off had brought him here to this glitzy, glorious, glamorous gambling town. His quarry was here.

The creature he had been searching for over many troublesome miles and nerve-fraught days, plus all at great expense. There the creature was. A jewel beetle, the very one he was after. The beetle was nearby the entrance of a gambling casino named The Triple Tricky.

Silas Mournmorrow shot off at once to nab his long-sought for prize. But was stopped in his tracks by a grubby looking groundling beetle.

"Got a dollar, buddy?" said the grubby one. "Got a dollar to spare for a poor down-and-outer?"

"I'm afraid I cannot help you," said Silas, turning to left and right in an effort to dodge out the path of this scruffy nuisance of an insect, pestering him at his supreme moment. One eye

never left the prize he was after, so deliciously and tantalizingly near to within his reach.

"I gambled away all my wages," whined the pathetic groundling beetle, side-stepping as the other side-stepped. "Gambled away my life savings too – and my home! You see before you a sad and sorry sight. I'm skint! Sold out! Flat broke!"

"I know how you feel," and Silas Mournmorrow probably did know how the other felt, considering the exorbitant expense of his recent travelling.

"Mister, I ain't a dollar to my name."

"What is your name?" enquired Silas Mournmorrow, intent now on humouring this sad spectacle of insecthood. Anything, to get rid of him.

"Donald Domuch Dolittle – er, sir." And decided to add, "Of Doorknob Drive, downtown Detroit."

"Well," began the other, delving down into pants' pocket for a dollar bill. Against his better judgement, against the high principles he had always maintained and represented, against his very instincts… he passed the note over. "Take this, Donald Domuch Dolittle of Doorknob Drive, downtown Detroit. You now have a dollar to your name."

Which was more than could be said for himself, for Silas Mournmorrow had in fact given away his last and only financial resource.

"Now if you will excuse me," he concluded rather mournfully, "I have a most pressing engagement, an important appointment to keep," eyes still fastened fixedly and unfalteringly on that precious figure ahead…

CHAPTER 42

Bertrand marched up and down before the entrance to the Triple Tricky Gambling Casino, impatiently waiting for Wally, who had disappeared inside at least an hour ago.

When he decided to wait no longer and go in to drag Wally from the premises, out popped the wasp. Wally seemed as happy as a fly stuck in a jam-pot.

"You took your time in that – that place!" Bertrand blasted him. "What in goodness have you been up to in there? And why are you grinning like a demented idiot?"

"Oh, nothing in particular," said the wasp cheerily. "Just enjoying things in general. I like it here, I really do."

"What have you been up to?" repeated Bertrand with some heat. "Spending all that precious time in what I consider a horrid den of… well, whatever."

"Oh, nothing in particular."

"Then why the massive grin?"

"Nothing in particular, nothing at all. Just this and that, you know?"

"No, I do not know."

"Actually, I got talking to a Nevada wasp. Hadd Chance is his name. He saw me observing things and said, 'No chance.'"

"No chance of what?"

"Oh things, you know?"

"No, I do not know."

"Then Hadd's brother showed up and joined us. Larst, he's called."

"Larst Chance?"

"That's him! Do you know him?"

"In course I do not know him. How could I know him or of him?"

"Well, Larst said the same thing as his brother."

"Larst Chance said 'No chance'?"

"That's it, you've hit the nail on the tail."

"I beg your pardon?"

"The head, the head I said, or meant to say."

"Hmm, well, it does not explain the reason for that ludicrously silly grin on your face."

Bertrand's attention was then taken by something else.

"Why are you hiding what looks like a sack behind your back? What, might I ask, have you got in that sack and how did you come by it?"

"Just something I picked up in the casino."

"I also asked what have you in it?"

"In this sack?"

"In course I mean in that sack! Gracious, you exasperate me at times, you truly do!"

"Nothing in particular," replied Wally, still foolishly grinning.

A shadow of a sudden fell upon Bertrand…

CHAPTER 43

Bertrand glanced up to be confronted by a tall, dark, imposing figure, bearing an essentially severe and austere expression on his face.

"Would I be correct in saying, sir," murmured the stranger in solemn tones, "that I am addressing Bertrand-Bartholomew Beetle Esquire?"

"I am that beetle, yes."

Bertrand was puzzled, curious, intrigued – all in short order. Had he met this creature before, who appeared vaguely familiar?

Silas Mournmorrow introduced himself, and went into further detail concerning his station in life, or rather his professional standing:

"I am, sir, an accredited representative of Lucky Dip Dunkles, the Lucky Dip Raffles and Lottery Department."

"Ah, in course!" exclaimed Bertrand, now recognising this tall, black-hatted, black-caped beetle. "I remember thinking at the time of your visit that you might be a funeral caretaker or even maybe a tax inspector. My apologies for so assuming such silly imaginings."

"Of no matter, sir, of no consequence. Now, sir, you confirm your place of residence as 32A Beech Tree House, of Lower Tinklewigglebottom in the county, the **English** county, of… Picklepompshire, is it?"

As Silas said this, he glanced sideways at the wasp, who was grinning at him like one half demented. *What a curious fellow!*

Bertrand verified the truth of the other's statement with an emphatic though suspicious nod. He did not know what or where this enquiry was leading to, but felt uneasy about it.

"Furthermore," continued Silas relentlessly, "at 32**B** Beech Tree House resides one Barry-Bartok-Barnacle Bubblesworth Beetle… er, hum, Esquire?"

"That is correct. My good neighbour and friend Barry, yes. But tell me, what exactly is the purpose of your business?"

"It is business of an imperative nature, sir," said Silas in his usual mournful tone of voice. "It falls to me… it is my unpleasant duty to inform you that a dreadful mistake has been made – No, sir, not of your making, I hasten to add – but of the company I represent; that is, Lucky Dip Dunkles."

"In what respect or manner has a mistake been made?" A cold feeling of dread passed through Bertrand. "And how or why does it concern me?"

Silas Mournmorrow was momentarily distracted by the wildly grinning wasp before him. He shrugged and pressed on : "You, sir," again addressing the beetle, "you should in actual fact have received a grand consolation prize, while your close neighbour Barry-Bartok-Barnacle Bubblesworth should by rights be awarded the cash prize of ten thousand faldooshes."

"Oh dear! Oh my Aunt Eliza! Oh goodness gracious!"

Bertrand was utterly devastated, shot to pieces!

"It is my painful duty therefore," continued the other, relentlessly as before. "I am required by my company directors to firmly demand that you return this prize fund fully and forthwith."

"But – but it has all gone!" gasped Bertrand.

"I beg your pardon, sir, but did you say **all gone**?"

"All spent! Every bit of it. Well, apart from the necessary expenses that will certainly be needed for our homeward journey. A pocketful of change is all that is left, small change it is too."

Silas Mournmorrow was struck dumb, mortified, stupefied at this most awful revelation.

Bertrand and Wally were then utterly amazed as they watched the tall beetle's extraordinary weird antics. Silas threw his hat to the ground, stomped on it, yelling out with a voice of acute desperation:

"My creditors will be my predators!
"They'll snatch back credit and loans
"And cause no end of storm and strife!
"They'll take the very coping stones
"Of my wall of Life;
"So what chance is there for hope
"When even coping stones cannot cope?"

"My dear fellow," said Bertrand in soothing tones, "don't take on so. Life is not worth it."

"Life is not worth anything! Not now! I am destitute! Bankrupt! Ready for the Workhouse! The Treadmill! I am ruined! RUINED!"

"Do have a care, dear soul, go easy on yourself, I beg of it."

Bertrand had at last sussed out the infantile behaviour of his old friend. He turned to the still madly grinning wasp, giving a compassionate look, which suddenly switched to a more meaningful kind of look.

"I am sure we can help out in some way, can we not, Wallace?" That meaningful look still prominent there on his noble countenance. "Do you think we can help this poor fellow in perhaps a pecuniary way?"

"Per… per… *per-coonery?*"

"Yes, pecuniary. In short, financial, monetary, moneywise, cash-wise and no dollar dilly dallying."

That hit home. Hit hard.

That wiped the grin off Wally's face.

"Well, my dear Wallace, what do you say? Oh, nothing at all is it?"

CHAPTER 44

"Come now, tell me," pressured Bertrand, "how much have you won?"

Wally's grin returned, disappeared again, and returned once more for a fleeting moment. He stared blankly at his friend as though he had been spoken to in a foreign language.

"What makes you think I have won anything?" he stalled, dodging the issue.

Bertrand spluttered with laughter. "Why, you wily creature, you have dollar signs stamped on your eyeballs! Now I understand the phrase *'stinking rich'*, because you positively **reek** of money. Is not that so? And there is yet an explanation for the sack you are holding tight to like it is your life's worth. Now do be a good fellow and tell me exactly how much you have won."

"You wouldn't believe me if I told you," countered the careful, cautious wasp.

"I think I shall. I am certain I shall. You *know* I shall."

"Okay, I will."

"You will what?"

"Tell you what my winnings are, the full round sum and no cheating on numbers."

"Go on then, I am listening…"

"I shall have to whisper it. I insist."

"Very well, if you insist. So go on then, I am still listening…"

"I have won… Hee-hee-hee! I have here in this sack…"

"Yes… ?"

"Forty thousand dollars!"

"FORTY THOU – !"

"Shush, quiet please! That's the sum total."

"My goodness gracious, Wallace!"

"Surprised you, hey?"

"Hmm…" deliberated Bertrand, and trying not to show a crafty look which crept up on him out of nowhere. "You know, my dear old friend, half of that is equal to ten thousand faldooshes…"

"The exact sum I suppose you expect me to part with. Am I right or am I right?"

"Well, it would make a magnificent and generous gesture to pay back that poor tall soul moping there, and put him out of his misery."

"But then I shall be miserable, doubly so," complained Wally.

"You would still have the equivalent of ten thousand faldooshes left, won't you? Is that not enough?"

Wally now deliberated, or at any rate pretended to deliberate, and finally said, "Yes, of course, you're right, Bertie. Can't be too greedy, can we? Win a bit, lose a bit, what's the difference? Only a *bit*."

"Yours is a lofty soul, Wallace Warrington," smiled Bertrand, which pleased his friend enormously. "So give the poor chap the money. Give it to him now."

"Before I change my mind?"

"You would not stoop so low, would not ever do such an underhand thing, you are an insect of high honour."

CHAPTER 45

Silas Mournmorrow was of course delighted and grateful to get back the full sum of prize money, though it was hard to tell the gratefulness with that perpetually sad, unhappy face of his.

Something bothered Bertrand afterwhile, catching a certain thought that popped into his active beetle brain. He gazed keenly up at the tall black beetle.

"By the way, sir," he opened up coolly, "what is that grand consolation prize you mentioned and to which I am presumably now entitled?"

"Oh, er… hum," faltered Silas in some embarrassment, "the consolation prize…"

He was assuredly and pointedly embarrassed, but Bertrand gave him no quarter, in fact he gave him a hard cold look, and said:

"Well?" (said coldly)

"Actually…"

"Yes?" pursued Bertrand icily.

"As it happens…"

"Yes?" (said frostily)

"Well, you see..."

"Well?"

"To put it plainly..."

"Please do!"

At last, Silas gave in. "The Consolation Prize is, my dear sir and generous benefactor," he half mumbled in grave tones, "is, with much forethought and planning... A TRIP FOR TWO TO LAS VEGAS!"

Bertrand and Wally exchanged looks.

Said Wally: "I hadn't heard of that B4."

Said Bertrand: "Bee Four?"

Said Wally: "No, **before**!"

Said Bertrand: "Oh! Ah! Hmm..."

Their eyes met, twinkling and sparkling with suppressed humour.

Then they fell to the ground, rolling about and roaring helplessly with unfettered laughter.

While Silas Mournmorrow simply stared on, as forlorn as a windflown fallen flower... staring mournfully.

"Now wait a moment," he mused momentarily to himself, "there is much more to life than just misery, moping and moroseness, for there is also – dare I think it? – there is also happiness and there is jollity and there is hilarity, is there not?"

Something quite untoward happened next. This normally morbid, miserable morsel of an insect realised in one swift flash that being mournful or miserable was not at all necessary nor needful, not now. It was out of fashion. It was out the window. A small crack appeared on his doleful face. The crack widened. His mouth widened in an upward direction.

And there it was! Silas was actually smiling! Smiling

sweetly and serenely. Yes, it was definitely a genuine smile! When at last he finally caught the humour of those two happy carefree insects wriggling about with uncontrolled laughter, when he at last realised what joy and fun there is to be had in life, and living life to the full, to the uppermost, to Cloud Nine in all its grand glory, Silas too dropped to the ground, joining Wally and Bertrand.

At first, like a baby finding it had a voice, he started with an untethered fit of giggles, later maturing to mad shrieks of laughter.

"Are you happy, Wally?"

"Oh brimfully, bathfully, Bertrand! Oceanfully!"

"Me too!" chortled Silas.

"Well," chuckled Bertrand, "carry on carrying on!"

Three joyful insects laughing and dancing on a dusty, sandy Las Vegas sidewalk, human beings passing by and totally unaware of their presence…

A BONUS CHAPTER

After a while, taking their leave of a deliriously happy Mr Mournmorrow, our notable – that is to say, our *noble* – duo set off into the sunset, Wally muttering Western cowboy style:

"An insect has gotta do what an insect has gotta do…"

Then, somewhat high-spiritedly, certainly joyfully, our wasp friend changed gear, thinking now of dear old England, and broke into song:

"*Oh! to go blackberrying on Buckbindleback Moor,*
"*Big fruity blackberries, blackberries galore!*
"*To get sozzled as a newt*
"*On that luscious juicy fruit,*
"*Then push on back and pick some more!*"

"You have a telling tentative talent, I tell you," said Bertrand a smidgen enviously. "Now, Wallace Warrington, what are you pointing at?"

"That view."

"Is that your point of view?"

"No, I was pointing *at* the view."

"I see your point."

"No you don't, I've stopped pointing."

"You have stopped *painting*? When did you *start* painting?"

"I started *panting* when I saw that scorpion."

"I take it that you do not particularly care for scorpions. Is that the case?"

"Well, no, not to socialise with, at any rate."

"Glad to hear it. Stick to your own kind, as old wise insects always say. Let us now direct our steps, dear Wallace, towards that wonderful sunset – What are you pointing at this time?"

"That view."

"I see."

"*Icy*? Not here in Arizona at this time of year."

"Well, dear soul, let us crack on, let us finish it off there…"

… As the beetle and the wasp continued on most amicably into a glorious desert sunset.

END

A SMIDGEN BIT EXTRA...

"Are you humming there, Bertrand?"

"Hmm, that precisely, Wallace my dear friend. I do like a Franck Sonata. Nothing that cheers the soul as much as a Franck Sonata, I do declare."

Wally glanced quizzically at his beetle companion. "Fronk Sinatra? Is he Classical?"

NOW IT'S THE END